This is how Tilly Mint began. When I was a little girl, my mum and dad used to call me Tilly Mint. It wasn't my real name, of course. We lived in a part of Liverpool called Knotty Ash, and all the other girls in the street were called Tilly Mint, too. We moved to the Wirral when I was four, and I still met Tilly Mints. I still do, but they always come from Liverpool. Years later, a Radio Sheffield producer called Dave Sheasby asked me to write some stories for young children, and I knew I wanted to write about a little girl called Tilly Mint. I used to tell my children stories about an old lady called Mrs Hardcastle, and I decided to put her in the Tilly Mint stories I was writing. It was only then that I discovered something wonderful about Mrs Hardcastle. She could make magic things happen.

The stories were broadcast many times on Radio Sheffield, and then published as my fourth book, *Tilly Mint Tales*. Then Ron Rose, who ran a theatre company called DAC, asked me to write a play about Tilly Mint to take around schools. I wrote a musical about Tilly Mint and Captain Cloud and the last dodo in the world. It was so popular that I made it into a short novel, *Tilly Mint and the Dodo*. It's lovely to see both my books brought together in this way, with Tony Ross's wonderful illustrations. I wonder if any little girls called Tilly Mint will read it!

Berlie Doherty

YOUNG CORGI

Young Corgi books are perfect when you are looking for great books to read on your own. They are full of exciting stories and entertaining pictures. There are funny books, scary books, spine-tingling stories and mysterious ones. Whatever your interests you'll find something in Young Corgi to suit you, from ponies to football, from families and friends to ghosts. The books are written by some of the most famous and popular of today's children's authors, and by some of the best new talents, too.

Whether you read one chapter a night, or devour the whole book in one sitting, you'll love Young Corgi Books. The more you read, the more you'll want to read!

Other Young Corgi Books to get your teeth into:

Annie and the Aliens by Emily Smith
Pigface by Catherine Robinson
Dogspell by Helen Dunwoodie

www.berliedoherty.com

Tilly Mint Tales

Berlie Doherty

Illustrated by Tony Ross

For Jean and Alan,
Ian, Beverley and Charlotte

TILLY MINT TALES
A YOUNG CORGI BOOK : 978 0552 54870 0

First published in Great Britain in two separate volumes
by Methuen Children's Books

Methuen editions published 1984, 1988
Young Corgi edition published 2003

7 9 10 8 6

The Random House Group Limited supports The Forest Stewardship Council (FSC), the
leading international forest certification organisation. All our titles that are printed on
Greenpeace approved FSC certified paper carry the FSC logo. Our paper procurement policy
can be found at www.rbooks.co.uk/environment.

Mixed Sources
Product group from well-managed
forests and other controlled sources
www.fsc.org Cert no. TT-COC-2139
© 1996 Forest Stewardship Council

Set in 14/16pt Bembo Schoolbook

Corgi Books are published by Random House Children's Books,
61–63 Uxbridge Road, London W5 5SA,
A division of The Random House Group Ltd

Addresses for companies within The Random House Group Limited can be
found at: www.randomhouse.co.uk/offices.htm

THE RANDOM HOUSE GROUP Limited Reg. No. 954009
www.kidsatrandomhouse.co.uk

A CIP catalogue record for this book is available from the British Library.

Printed in the UK by CPI Bookmarque, Croydon, CR0 4TD

Contents

TILLY MINT TALES

Tilly Mint
and the Leaf-lords

I don't know if you've ever met Tilly Mint.
She lives in one of those houses just up the
hill from the park. She's about as old as you,
I should think.

When Tilly's mum goes out to work, Mrs
Hardcastle from up the street pops in to look
after her. You must have seen *her*. She has
curly, white hair and pink cheeks. She has
shiny, blue, remembery sort of eyes, and
fidgety, talky sort of hands, and she's very old.
Very old. She once told Tilly that she was the
oldest woman in the world.

Now, there are two special things about
Mrs Hardcastle that you ought to know. The
first thing is, she's always dropping off to
sleep. Always. Easy as winking. She just closes
her eyes, and opens her mouth, and off she
goes. She snores too, sometimes. You should
hear her. And the second special thing is this:
when she goes to sleep, something magic
always seems to happen to Tilly Mint. Tilly
never says very much about it to Mrs
Hardcastle, and Mrs Hardcastle never says
very much about it to Tilly. It just happens,
and that's that. It's magic.

Like the time Tilly Mint saw the leaf-lords.
It happened on October the fifth.

Tilly was staring out of the window,
daydreaming, and waiting for her mum to
come home, when Mrs Hardcastle said:

"Well, Tilly Mint. Are you coming or not?"

Tilly jumped from her chair and pulled on
her duffel coat. "Where to, Mrs Hardcastle?"
she asked. "Where are we going?"

"Don't you ever listen, child? We're going
down to the park till your mum gets home
from work. Though how I'm going to get that
far in these new shoes I don't know. You might
have to give me a piggy-back, Tilly Mint."

They walked down the hill towards the
park, and as they got away from the road
and into the trees, the piles of dead leaves
grew higher and higher. Tilly scrunched
through them. The noise her feet made in the
leaves sounded like fifty fires burning. They
sounded like a hundred horses munching hay.

"It sounds as if you're walking through a
bag of broken biscuits, Tilly," said Mrs
Hardcastle. "What a row. Ah, but will you
look at those leaves dancing."

And as they stood under the trees, the
brown and green and golden and red and
orange and yellow leaves floated down

around them. Tilly thought it was one of the best days ever. But for some reason, Mrs Hardcastle thought it was one of the saddest days she could remember.

"I shall have to have a lie down, Tilly Mint," she said. "It's no good. I'm feeling right dopey." Mrs Hardcastle often felt dopey before her tea.

There was a bench nearby, and she sat herself down on it. She undid her new shoes, and took them off, and put them next to a pile of dead leaves. Then she lay down on the bench, with her handbag under her head, and her feet sticking over the end.

"I'll just have five minutes," she promised, yawning.

Tilly sighed. "But what shall I do, Mrs Hardcastle?" she asked.

"You could look for the leaf-lords," Mrs Hardcastle yawned. "Only don't tread on them, will you, love? And see if you can find some of their treasure . . ."

And then, as she said that, her voice sort of fizzled out into an enormous yawn, and then into a snore, and then into a lovely long whistle. Mrs Hardcastle was fast asleep. And Tilly Mint was bored.

Leaf-lords? she thought. What are they?

She sat for a long time listening to Mrs Hardcastle whistling away like a blackbird, and watching the leaves, and she said:

"What a lovely day it would be, if only something would happen!"

It was then that she thought she heard a whispery sort of voice saying,

"Spin around, swing around,
Float and flutter down,
Swirl around, twirl around . . ."

over and over again, in a crackly sort of crunched-up-paper-bag way.

It couldn't have been Mrs Hardcastle, could it, talking in her sleep? No. She was much too busy snoring and whistling to say anything like that. It couldn't have been the blackbird, could it, hiding in the branches at the top of the tree? No. He was much too busy singing up to the sunshine to say anything like that.

Tilly listened. There it was again!

"Spin around, swing around,
Float and flutter down,
Swirl around, twirl around . . ."

Tilly jumped off her bench in great excitement. It couldn't be the leaf-lords, could it? Could it?

She followed the sound of the paper-bag voice to the pile of dead leaves that were at the side of Mrs Hardcastle's bench, and just underneath her sticking-out feet. She poked about in them, and then pushed them to one side, and it was there, in the middle of the pile, that she found the leaf-lords.

Do you know what they looked like? They were seven little men; one in a brown cloak and one in a red one; one in an orange cloak and one in a green one; one in a golden cloak; one in a yellow cloak, and the littlest one of all was in a cloak of all these colours.

"Are you the leaf-lords?" whispered Tilly.

For an answer they leapt up, one by one, and as Tilly lifted the dead leaves away from them they began to dance, and they danced and sang to a wonderful whistling tune, and the amazing thing was that the wonderful whistling tune seemed to be coming from Mrs Hardcastle, lying there fast asleep in the bench.

"Leaf-lords leaping,
Spin around, swing around.
Leaf-lords leaping,

Float and flutter down.
Leaf-lords leaping,
Swirl around, twirl around.
Lovely leap-lords leap."

Tilly wanted to dance and sing with them!
Then she noticed that the leaf-lords were
dancing in a ring round Mrs Hardcastle's new,
brown, lace-up shoes. Tilly put them on,
without even taking her own off, and before
she'd had time to fasten them she was leaping
and jumping round with the leaf-lords, as
high as them, and as fast as them, and singing
the leaf-lords' song to the wonderful whistling
tune that seemed to be coming from Mrs
Hardcastle's mouth. Spinning and swinging
and dancing and prancing and swirling and
twirling and whizzing and whirling . . .
    Tilly noticed that everywhere the leaf-lords
danced there were little prickly balls in the
grass, like spiky apples, like tiny, round, green
hedgehogs, and every green spiky
hedgehoggy ball had a slit in it, and
something as brown and warm and shiny as
an eye gleamed inside the slit.
    "Lovely!" said Tilly, bending down to have
a closer look, and as she did so an ice-cold
shadow fell across her. She looked up, shivering.

The leaf-lords were still dancing, but in a
tearing, miserable, hunched-up sort of way.
The whistle still whistled, but in a sharp,
shrill, howling sort of way. The sun still shone,
but it was as cold as winter. And all the
colours of the sky and the trees and the leaves
and the grass seemed to have slipped away
into grey.

"What's happened?" asked Tilly. "Where's
the lovely day gone to?"

The leaf-lords scurried round Tilly's feet.

"The Cold Queen of Winter!" they screamed. "Too early! Too soon! Send her away! Send her away!"

Tilly could hear the Cold Queen of Winter cackling like broken twigs. She could feel her icy fingers and the chill of her damp breath on her skin.

"Too early! Too early!" the leaf-lords screamed. Tilly could feel all the brown eyes in the grass watching her.

"Don't worry, leaf-lords!" she said. "I'll get rid of her for you!"

She saw the Cold Queen of Winter's shadow flickering towards the trees, sending all the birds away in fright. Tilly bent down quickly and scooped up handfuls of the prickly green balls and flung them at the shadow.

"Scram!" she shouted. "We don't want you here yet!"

The leaf-lords danced round her, guiding her to where more of the green prickly balls lay. The Queen's shadow dodged through the trees, growing smaller and smaller as Tilly pelted her.

"And don't come back till November!" Tilly cried.

One by one, the birds flew back into the trees, and began to sing again. The sun and the sky and the trees and the leaves and the grass glowed with colour. As the howls of the banished Queen grew fainter and fainter, the lovely whistly tune started up, and the leaf-lords danced with joy. And everywhere on the grass, wherever Tilly had thrown them, all the prickly balls had split right open. Inside every one of them was another ball, gleaming brown and bright and beautiful.

Tilly danced round, scooping them up to put in her pockets, when suddenly . . . the wonderful whistle turned into a snore. Then a yawn. Mrs Hardcastle sat up on the bench. Tilly stood still. The leaf-lords lay like old brown leaves on the ground. Not a sound. Not a sound.

"Tilly Mint! Just what do you think you're doing in my shoes?" said Mrs Hardcastle. "Just look at my toes! They're like a bunch of frozen sausages!"

Tilly took the shoes off, and gave them to Mrs Hardcastle.

"I saw the leaf-lords, Mrs Hardcastle," she said, as they trudged back across the grass to the park gates.

"'Course you did." Mrs Hardcastle held

Tilly's hand very tightly. "Come on, Tilly Mint. Your mum will be wondering where we've got to, won't she?"

They climbed slowly back up the hill, and Tilly thought it was one of the nicest days she'd ever had. But Mrs Hardcastle was a bit sad, because it was a long time since she'd danced with the leaf-lords. A long, long time.

"Look," said Tilly, suddenly remembering what she'd found. "These will cheer you up, Mrs Hardcastle. Look what I've got in my pockets."

"Conkers!" laughed Mrs Hardcastle. "Tilly Mint! Conkers! You've found the treasure! Ooh, just wait till we get home. We'll thread them on string . . . and we'll have a conker-fight. Come on! Quick!"

She was so excited that she started running, in her new shoes. Tilly Mint smiled to herself, because she'd already had a conker-fight that day, hadn't she?

And she had won.

Tilly Mint
Learns to Fly

One wild and windy day, when Mum was taking Tilly Mint round to Mrs Hardcastle's for a couple of hours, the wind was so strong that it nearly blew them away. Tilly Mint clung onto Mum's hand as tight as she could, and Mum pulled her as hard as she could, but they didn't seem to get very far at all.

"Come on, Tilly!" Mum kept saying. "We'll never get there at this rate."

Tilly pushed with all her strength against the wind, and the wind pushed with all its strength against Tilly.

"I wish I could push the wind away!" gasped Tilly, when she had enough breath left to speak. "What good is it anyway?"

"Never mind," Mum said. "We're here now. You'll be nice and cosy in Mrs Hardcastle's kitchen, and I'll see you at tea time."

But Mrs Hardcastle didn't think much of that idea at all.

"We're not staying indoors on a day like this, Tilly Mint," she said. "Oh no, we're not wasting this wind!"

And Tilly had to put her duffel coat back on, and her scarf and her gloves and her bobble hat, even though she'd only just taken them off.

"Tie my laces up for me, Tilly," said Mrs Hardcastle. She couldn't bend down that far these days. "Will you just listen to the wind in the chimney!"

"Wouldn't it be nice to stay in and listen to it?" said Tilly hopefully.

But Mrs Hardcastle shook her head. "Never," she said. "Never, never, never.

The specialest thing in the whole world wide
Is the whistling wind when it's blowing wild.

"Remember that, Tilly Mint." Then she banged on the side of the budgie cage so that sleepy Mr Feathers fell off his perch and fluttered his wings in surprise. Two little blue feathers floated down.

"It was a day like today," Mrs Hardcastle said, "a day just like this, that I learned to fly. But that was years and years and years ago." She looked a little bit excited, and a little bit sad, because she was the oldest woman in the world, and she'd done so many things, so long ago.

"Anyway," she said, giving Tilly one of the little blue feathers from the bottom of the budgie cage, and keeping the other one for herself, "just you hang onto that, Tilly Mint. You might just need it. You never know what might happen, on a day like this. Remember what I told you."

"The specialest thing in the whole world wide
Is the whistling wind when it's blowing wild,"

whispered Tilly to herself. And out they went.

The wind grabbed them by the hair. It pulled their arms up the street. It pushed their legs down the street. Then it let go. Tilly sat down with a thump. The little blue feather was still safe in her hand. She clung onto Mrs Hardcastle's coat with the other hand, and pressed her bobble hat down with her fist. She closed her eyes, and battled on. Sometimes her legs went backwards, and sometimes they went forwards, and sometimes they didn't go at all. But Mrs Hardcastle staggered on till they got to the very top of the hill.

"This is just the sort of thing we need!" shouted Mrs Hardcastle excitedly. "A bangy whizzy whistly wind like this. This should do it.

"The specialest thing in the whole world wide
Is the whistling wind when it's blowing wild.
Spin in a circle, spread your arms high,
And see if the wind will make you fly!"

She started running round and round on the top of the hill, holding her blue feather high up in the air. You should have seen her! Her coat was flapping up right above her knees, and she didn't care! Her scarf wound itself off her neck and blew away, and she didn't care! Her hair flopped like a bush round her face, and she didn't care! Round and round she ran, and round and round ran the blue feather in her fingers.

"Come on, Tilly Mint!" she shouted. "Hold up your feather, and run!"

So Tilly Mint ran round and round after Mrs Hardcastle, holding her blue feather up in the air, and all of a sudden two things happened. Mrs Hardcastle stopped running round, and sat down very suddenly on the bench by the bus shelter; and Tilly Mint . . .

started to fly!

She wasn't just floating; she was really flying! Over the bus shelter, over the trees, over her street, over her house, over her park, and away, and away, and away.

The specialest thing in the whole world wide
Is the whistling wind when it's blowing wild.
Spin in a circle, hold your arms high
And see if the wind will make you fly.
Spin in a circle, spin in a ring,
Spin like a bird with your little blue wing,
And you're up where the clouds are,
You're tossed and you're twirled,
You're up where the birds are —
You're over the world!

When Tilly looked down again, she couldn't see her house, or her street, or even the hill. She was somewhere else! She was floating down, down, down towards sparkling blue rivers and bright green trees.

She could see brown children splashing in the water. She could hear a harsh grating sound, like the sound of someone sawing wood, and as she floated closer she could see that the sound was coming from a big-eared teddy-bear that was climbing slowly up a tree.

Tilly landed with a bump at the bottom of the tree, and one of the children ran to her, laughing, to help her up.

"Tilly Mint's come!" he called to the others.

"I saw a bear in that tree," Tilly told him.

"Koala!" the boy said. "He's a sleepy old thing. Don't bother about him. Come and play."

The children ran out of the trees and into a clearing. The ground was hard and yellow, like baked sand. The sun was hotter than Tilly had ever known it to be. No wonder these children don't wear many clothes, she thought. I do feel silly in my duffel coat and gloves and bobble hat.

"Take them off," the boy said. "Chuck them away."

"I'd better not," Tilly told him. "I'll need them for . . . when I go."

A terrible feeling was slowly creeping over her, like it does sometimes when you've done something wrong, or when you've forgotten something very important.

"My feather!" she gasped. "I've lost my feather! Now what do I do?"

There was a sudden heavy pounding over the ground. Three large animals came leaping

over the hard sand on their big back feet.
Bounce. BOUNCE. Bounce. BOUNCE.

"Kangaroos!" shouted the boy. "Look, Tilly.
Boomer, Flyer and Joey. And look what Flyer
has got in her pocket!"

Tilly knew all about pockets. That's where
you keep special things, she thought, feeling
in her own, like conkers and shells, and
maybe feathers? No. Not feathers.

But goodness knows what a kangaroo
would keep in hers. Flyer held her pocket
open, and Tilly peeped in and there, peering
back up at her, were the bright eyes of . . .
another kangaroo!

"A baby joey!" breathed the boy.
"Beautiful!"

"Can I ride one of them?" Tilly asked.

The boy laughed. "You could try. Couldn't
she, Boomer?"

Boomer squatted down and Tilly put her
arms round his neck and tried to swing her
legs round his haunches. Instantly Boomer
tucked his front arms in, stuck out his long tail,
and BOUNCED and bounded AND bounced and
TILLY clung ON to HIM as IF he WAS a ship AT
SEA and CLOSED her EYES tight. OH!

She slid off and picked herself up shakily.
"Thank you, Boomer," she said.

She had landed back by Koala's tree, and now she could hear a whistling and squawking in the branches above her.

"It's all right for you, laughing!" she said.

Dozens of little birds, bright as flowers, were bobbing among the branches . . . yellow ones, green ones, white ones, and one blue one.

"Aren't they . . . ?" Tilly began.

"Budgies," said the boy, who had run after her and Boomer. "Pretty birds."

The blue one fluttered off the branch onto Tilly's shoulder, and looked at her knowingly.

"Aren't you . . . you're ever so like . . . Mr Feathers?" Tilly asked.

The blue budgie copied her. "Mr Feathers? Mr Feathers?" He flew back into the tree to join the others, and as he did so one blue feather floated to the ground.

Tilly picked it up. The branches of the tree whooshed above her.

"The wind is coming!" shouted the boy. "Shelter! Shelter from the wind!"

But Tilly had no intention of sheltering from the wind. She ran right out into it, while the great trees bowed and twisted and the sand fizzed in clouds along the ground. She held up the blue feather. She clung onto her bobble hat with the other hand, and the wind lifted her up, up, past Koala, past the tops of the trees.

"Bye, Tilly Mint!"

"Goodbye, Boy!" shouted Tilly, and up she went, over the top of the world.

When she looked down again, she saw a little brown blob far, far below her, and she knew what it was. It was Mrs Hardcastle, fast asleep and snoring on the seat by the bus shelter.

She could also see a tiny bright thing beetling along like a ladybird, and she thought, That's a bus! Perhaps my mum's on it, coming home for tea. And here am I, stuck up here! I hope she won't be cross with Mrs Hardcastle for going to sleep and losing me like this!

Next minute, she started turning over in the air. She was floating down and down. Her tummy turned over inside her, all on its own. And then she felt her feet dragging on the ground, slower and slower and slower, and she stopped with a bump just by the bench where Mrs Hardcastle was having a doze.

Mrs Hardcastle opened her eyes with a jump.

"What's happened to you, Tilly Mint? Where've you been?"

Tilly looked round her. Everything was still again, even her tummy.

"I've been flying, Mrs Hardcastle," she said.

Mrs Hardcastle sighed. She still had her feather in her hand. She put it away in her handbag.

"I used to fly, long ago," she said. "When I was a little girl."

"Mrs Hardcastle, where do budgies come from?"

"Budgies? Like Mr Feathers? From Australia, Tilly. Pretty bird, that's what budgerigar means. It's the only Australian word I know, apart from koala, and kangaroo . . . why, what ever are you laughing at, Tilly Mint? You're not going to tell me you flew to Australia, are you?"

But Tilly didn't say a word, because the bus came up to the stop, and her mum got off, and they all went home for tea.

When the Cock Crows

Mr Pig has slept in Tilly Mint's bed, just under her head, for about six years. No wonder he's a bit squashed. Tilly doesn't very often take him out with her in case she loses him, but yesterday Mrs Hardcastle told Tilly to bring Mr Pig to her house, and to bring her wellies too.

"Are we going out somewhere?" Tilly asked.

"No," said Mrs Hardcastle. "I'm going to make some coconut buns."

Tilly loved Mrs Hardcastle's coconut buns. They were all crunchy on the outside, and chewy in the middle, and sometimes they had a red-and-sticky cherry on the top.

"Why did I have to bring my wellies then?" asked Tilly, as Mrs Hardcastle hunted for her mixing bowl.

Mrs Hardcastle shook her head. "Can't remember, Tilly," she said. "I just thought they might come in useful."

"And why did I have to bring Mr Pig?"

asked Tilly. "He'd be much better off in bed, where it's warm."

"I can't remember that either," said Mrs Hardcastle. "But I'm sure we'll find out. Look, Tilly, I thought you might like to do some making, while I do my baking. I've put out some boxes, and some plasticine, and some paints. I should think you can make something with that lot."

Tilly was a bit fed up. She wasn't keen on making. She liked doing. And she'd rather go out somewhere than stay in, any day.

"Silly boxes!" she grumbled, as she cut a hole in the biggest one and stuck some paper over it for a door. "Stupid green paint!" she complained, as she painted three sheets of paper. "Smelly plasticine!" she moaned, as she rolled and moulded fifteen coloured shapes.

"Look, Mrs Hardcastle!" she said at last. "I've made a farm!"

Mrs Hardcastle came to have a look. She sat down on the floor with Tilly and looked at the green paper fields, and the cardboard farmhouse, and the barn, with its black-and-white blobby sheepdog.

She helped Tilly to stand the five plasticine cows up, as if they were waiting to be milked. She put the three pink, piggy blobs in a little carton, for a pig-sty. Then Tilly put five white sheep in the green field behind the barn. Mrs Hardcastle picked up the biggest plasticine shape.

"What's this?" she asked. "It looks like a half-eaten sausage, Tilly Mint."

"It's the farmer," said Tilly. "I can't do farmers."

Mrs Hardcastle shaped the sausage till it had two legs with black wellies on, and a white handkerchief hanging out of his pocket, and a smiling face.

"That's Farmer Heyday!" she said.

"Is it?" asked Tilly.

"Here's some matchsticks to make a gate," said Mrs Hardcastle. "It's nearly ready, Tilly."

"Is it?" asked Tilly.

"Pull me up," said Mrs Hardcastle. "I'm feeling right dozy. I'd better sit at the table and get this mixing done. Oh, don't forget the cock!

"When the cock crows,
Everyone knows
Day has begun –
Bring out the sun!

"Good job I remembered that, Tilly Mint."

She sat herself down at the table, and, with the last of the black plasticine, Tilly made a little black cock, and with a tiny bit of the red plasticine she made a little cresty comb for his head. She balanced the cock very carefully on its matchstick post, and as she was drawing her fingers away,

"Cock-a-doodle-doo!" He crowed!

"What?" said Tilly. She nearly dropped him, she was so surprised. She looked round for Mrs Hardcastle, but *she* was fast asleep and snoring, with her arms all covered in flour, and her hands in a bowl of coconut and sugar.

"I might have known!" said Tilly. "She's off again!"

The cock crowed again, and this time Tilly saw him stretch his neck and lift up the red comb on his head and open his beak as wide as it would go. He seemed to swell up with pride at the wonderful sound he was making.

"When the cock crows,
Everyone knows
Day has begun —
Bring out the sun!"

whispered Tilly Mint.

"Cock-a-doodle-doo!" The paper door that Tilly had stuck over the hole in the cardboard-box farmhouse opened, and out came Farmer Heyday. He stretched his brown plasticine arms, and whistled.

"Hey, Sheppa! Come on, Sheppa!" he called.

The black-and-white collie came out, stretching, from the barn, and barked hello to the farmer.

Tilly hardly dared breathe! She lay on her tummy with her nose pressed up against the matchstick gate, and Mr Pig snuggled up beside her. The farmer saw her, though. He strode across the paper yard, his plasticine knees bending just above the top of his black wellies, and Sheppa bounced on plasticine legs beside him.

"Well, are you coming in, or not?" Farmer Heyday shouted, peering through the bars of the matchstick gate. "You and that daft woolly pig?"

Tilly jumped. "Yes. No. If I can. I can't though. I'm too big."

Farmer Heyday snorted. "Suit yourself. But if you do come, put your wellies on!"

He strode off to the barn and led Tilly's cows in, one by one, to be milked. Tilly could hear their low, dark voices as they talked to each other in the shadows.

How she wanted to follow them! She took her slippers off and put on her wellies, and when she bent down to pick up Mr Pig again, she felt a strange rushing in her tummy, as if she was going down a slide, very fast, and she stood up . . . to find that her head was no higher than the gate of the farm! She could smell the farm – the hot, sweet, sharp smell of the dung the cows had dropped! She could smell the grass! She could feel it under her feet, springy and oozing with mud as she pushed open the gate.

As soon as she was inside the farmyard, Mr Pig started behaving like a pig! He

snorted and squealed in her arms, he wriggled
and kicked, till she had to drop him. He ran to
the wall of the pig-sty, jumped in, and there
he rolled over on his back in the mud with the
three other pigs, and lay, kicking his legs in
the air and snorting with utter happiness.

"Mr Pig! You'll be filthy!" said Tilly. "You
needn't think you're getting in my bed
tonight, looking like that!"

"Aren't they beautiful!" said Farmer
Heyday fondly, leaning over the pig-sty.
"Prettier than babies, pigs are. Give me pigs
any day."

"Can I play in that field by the barn?"
Tilly asked him. "I painted it myself!"

"Off you go then," said Farmer Heyday, a
bit puzzled. "But don't be long – you're
wanted in the kitchen. And there's new lambs
in that field – fresh as daisies, mind!"

Lambs! Tilly could hear them, even as she
was running to the stile, and she could see
them, all her little white plasticine blobs, all
turned into real, woolly, skippy, scuttery,
chewing, wobbly, bouncing, shouting,
coughing lambs. What a wonderful racket!

But the smell coming from the kitchen was
even more wonderful. It was the warm, sweet,
eggy smell of baking.

36

Mrs Heyday had her back turned as Tilly went in; she was bringing a tray of new buns from the oven.

"You'll have to have one of these before you go," she said, turning round. Tilly stared. She couldn't help it. Mrs Heyday looked just like . . . but she couldn't be. She had the same sort of remembery blue eyes as . . . but she couldn't have.

"You're like somebody I know," Tilly said at last.

"Am I?" Mrs Heyday smiled. "Have a coconut bun, Tilly Mint."

As Tilly was biting into her third coconut bun, all crunch on the outside, and chewy in the middle, with a red-and-sticky cherry on the top, she heard a jostling, rumbling, tumbling noise outside the window; a snorting, snuffling, scuffling sort of noise, full of squeaks and feet.

"What's that?" she whispered, in a coconutty voice.

Mrs Heyday wiped her eyes on her pinny. "It's the pigs," she said sadly. "Poor Mr Heyday! He hates market day. He has to take all his lovely pigs to market today, and sell them, every one!"

"Oh no!" gasped Tilly. She dropped the

cherry bit of her bun that she'd been saving for last, and ran out into the farmyard.

Farmer Heyday was standing by a cart, blowing his nose unhappily. Sheppa was leaping about and barking, and the pigs were running up a plank and into the cart that would take them off to market.

And right in the middle of them, covered in mud, was Mr Pig!

"Come back, Mr Pig!" Tilly shouted. "Don't go to market! You're not that sort of pig!"

She climbed into the cart, snatched up Mr Pig in both her arms, and ran out of the farmyard, through the gate – and onto Mrs Hardcastle's carpet.

And there she was, as high as the table again, and looking down at the little cardboard farmhouse, and the painted paper fields, and the plasticine animals, as still and silent as statues.

"Come on, Mr Pig," she whispered. "I'd better get these wellies off, and brush your mud away, before Mrs Hardcastle sees us."

And as she tiptoed out of the kitchen to do just that, Mrs Hardcastle opened her eyes and smiled, and carried on making her coconut buns.

Wonderful Worms

The day before yesterday, Tilly Mint and Mrs Hardcastle went down to the park to find some magic. They didn't say there were going to find some magic, but that's what Tilly thought. She felt it in her bones. The birds were singing brightly in the trees, and fetching and carrying things for their nests.

But all Mrs Hardcastle seemed to be interested in was worms.

"Just look at that worm, Tilly!" she said, when they walked past a bed of earth that had just been turned. "Just look at that blobby old worm!"

Tilly didn't like worms. "Eugh!" she said. "I'm not going near a worm."

Mrs Hardcastle was surprised. "I thought everyone liked worms, Tilly Mint," she said. "Worms arc wonderful.

"How they wibble, and they wobble,
and they wubble all around,
How they dibble, and they dabble,

And they double up and down.
How they're pink, and how they're pokey,
How they pull across the ground,
How they wind, and how they wander,
How they wiggle round and round!"

"Not to me, they're not," said Tilly. "That worm's got nowhere to go. He looks bored. He's like a piece of string without a parcel."

"He's like a shoelace looking for a shoe," laughed Mrs Hardcastle.

"He's like a piece of spaghetti that nobody wants to eat," said Tilly Mint.

"Don't you be so sure about that!" Mrs Hardcastle said. "Somebody wants to eat him. Look!"

Just above them, on the branch of a high tree, sat a little brown bird, singing his head off. His eyes were as bright as buttons. He was watching the worm. Suddenly he flew down from the branch, and he hopped across to where the worm was wriggling about with nowhere to go, looking bored.

"Look out!" shouted Mrs Hardcastle to the worm. But she was too late. The hoppity bird had put his beak right round the worm. The worm tried to wriggle back down into the earth. The brown bird dug his feet in, and pulled and pulled and pulled. The pink worm stretched and stretched and stretched.

And, POP! Out came the worm. The brown bird fell over; then he stood up, shook his feathers, and flew off with the worm waving helplessly in his beak.

"Hooray!" Mrs Hardcastle clapped her hands.

Now it was Tilly who was surprised. "I thought you liked worms, Mrs Hardcastle," she said.

"So I do," Mrs Hardcastle said. "But I like birds more. Just think of those little baby birds all snug and warm in their nest, waiting for their tea. They'll be very pleased when they see that worm."

I wouldn't mind being a baby bird, all snug and warm in a nest, thought Tilly. But I'd jump right out of it if anyone gave me worms for my tea. Fancy eating a worm!

"I nearly ate a worm once, Tilly Mint, when I was a little girl. But oh, that was so long ago. That was years and years and years ago. I've nearly forgotten all about it."

And when Mrs Hardcastle said that, it was in her drowsy, far-away, remembery sort of voice, and her eyes seemed to be looking into long, long ago. Then she sat down on a park bench, and she fell asleep.

"Crumbs!" said Tilly. "I'm in for it now! Magic time!"

She closed her eyes, and when she opened them, she was in a dark, dark place. She seemed to be in a tiny, little, dark room, with hard, smooth, warm walls, and it was round.

"No, it isn't!" said Tilly, after a bit. "It's not round! It's egg-shaped. I must be . . . inside . . . an egg!"

She pushed her head up against the top of her egg, and the shell began to crack. She pushed her arms out against the sides of her egg, and the shell began to crunch. She pushed her feet out through the bottom of her egg, and the shell began to crack, crunch, crumble.

And she was out into the air, into the sunshine, into the lovely blue light that was full of the song of birds.

Tilly took a deep breath and looked round her. Three fluffy birds were standing next to her, blinking in the sunlight. They were all standing on bits of shell. And underneath the bits of shell, there was straw, and grass, and twigs, and leaves, all plaited together like a warm, snug hat. They were in a nest!

Tilly hopped to the side of it and looked down. The nest seemed to be right at the top of the highest tree in the world. The branches began to sway in the wind.

"I'm hungry!" cheeped all the baby birds. "Very hungry."

So am I! thought Tilly. Very, very hungry.

Just then, the brown bird hopped onto the side of the nest. Tilly recognized him by his eyes that were as bright as buttons, and by his dirty feet, and by the pink worm that was wriggling about in his beak. The baby birds pushed each other over in excitement.

Tilly remembered what Mrs Hardcastle had told her about the wonderful worms:

"How they wibble, and they wobble,
And they wubble all around,

How they dibble, and they dabble,
And they double up and down.
How they're pink, and how they're pokey,
How they pull across the ground,
How they wind, and how they wander,
How they wiggle round and round!"

The brown bird saw that Tilly had her beak open, and he hopped over to her and started to lower the worm into her beak!

"Oh no!" said Tilly. "I'm not that hungry! I'm not having worms for my tea!"

She took the poor old worm very gently into her beak, and climbed up onto the side of the nest. She looked down from the top of the highest tree in the world.

"Bird in a nest on a branch in a tree,
Sail in the wind like a ship on the sea.
Worm in the beak of the bird in the skies,
Point to the ground, and close your eyes!"

Tilly Mint spread out her fluffy, feathery arms, and she closed her eyes that were as bright as buttons, and she jumped. She floated down, and down, and down.

And when she opened her eyes again, she was standing on the soft, brown earth with the little, pink worm in her hand. She knelt down and put him on the earth.

"In you go, little worm," she whispered. "You pop down there, and don't come out again till night-time."

The worm tucked his head into the soil and slithered out of sight.

Tilly remembered Mrs Hardcastle, fast asleep and snoring in the sunshine. She shook her arms to make quite sure there were no feathers left on, and then she woke her up.

"Wake up, Mrs Hardcastle!" she said. "I'm ever so hungry."

Mrs Hardcastle opened her eyes. She looked at the blue sky, which was full of birdsong. She looked up at the branches of the tallest tree in the world, and saw, at the very top, a little nest, swaying in the wind like a boat on the sea. She looked at the brown birds, busy with their fetching and carrying.

"Hello, Tilly Mint!" she said. And then she said: "Let's go home, shall we, and have spaghetti for our tea."

And they did.

Lions Are Lovely

Last night, Mrs Hardcastle came round to keep an eye on Tilly while her mum was at the supermarket. They talked about goblins and then about ghosts and then Mrs Hardcastle said:

"Tilly Mint, are you scared of anything?"

Tilly thought very hard. "No, I don't think so," she said. "Only lions. I think I'm a little bit scared of lions."

Mrs Hardcastle looked surprised. "Lions! Fancy being scared of them! Have you ever seen a lion, Tilly."

"No," said Tilly. "I don't think so. Not a real one. But I think I'd be scared of one if I did."

"That's crackers, Tilly Mint," said Mrs Hardcastle. "Crackers. Lions are lovely. I saw a real lion once, years and years ago. I wasn't a bit scared of it. In fact, do you know what I did?"

"No," said Tilly. "What did you do, Mrs Hardcastle?"

"I . . ." Mrs Hardcastle began, and then she stopped. "No, I'll tell you later what I did. Put the telly on, Tilly. There's a jungle film on. There might just be a lion in that."

Tilly switched on the television. The jungle film was just beginning. She settled herself on her favourite rug, with its lovely, soft, silky strands, as gold-and-red as any lion's head. Mrs Hardcastle stretched herself comfortably on the settee behind her.

"By the way, Tilly," she murmured sleepily. "This programme finishes at six o'clock. You won't forget that, will you?"

It was a wonderful programme. Tilly saw snakes, and monkeys and giraffes. She saw elephants crashing through the trees. She saw tiny little birds as bright as jewels. And, suddenly, she saw the lion. Its huge head seemed to fill the whole screen. It seemed to be looking straight at Tilly. It roared.

"Lions are lovely," muttered Mrs Hardcastle, half-asleep. "As gentle as milk."

The lion roared again, and Tilly said nervously:

"Lions are lovely,
As gentle as milk.
Brighter than flames,
And smoother than silk."

47

As soon as Tilly said that, the lion stepped right out of the television screen, onto Tilly's carpet. It was bigger than the armchair. It was brighter than the fire. It was the most beautiful creature that Tilly had ever seen. She looked round to tell Mrs Hardcastle, but she was fast asleep on the settee, and snoring, very gently.

Lion roared softly.

Tilly tiptoed over to him and stroked his back. It felt as soft and silky as her favourite rug. His eyes were as golden as sunshine.

"Lions are lovely," whispered Tilly.
"As gentle as milk.
Brighter than flames,
And smoother than silk.
Lions are lovely,
Wild things and free,
As fast as the wind is,
As strong as the sea."

Lion crouched down. Tilly climbed onto his back. And instantly, they were away! Lion leapt through the open window, with Tilly clinging onto his mane. They were in the street, with cars rushing past and people shouting.

"It's a lion! Look at that lion!" shouted Tilly's neighbours. "Look at Tilly Mint on his back!"

Tilly knew where her lion would like to be. She tugged on his long bright mane. "Go down the hill, Lion!" she shouted. "Down to the park."

Lion bounded down the hill. Tilly gripped him tightly.

"Look, look, look at the lion!" the birds cried, dancing over their heads. "Look at the lovely lion!"

As soon as Lion reached the park, he streaked like fire across the grass. His long legs hardly seemed to touch the ground. His mane streamed like strands of gold. He roared with joy.

"Lions are lovely," laughed Tilly Mint.
"As gentle as milk.
Brighter than flames,
And smoother than silk.
Lions are lovely,
Wild things and free,
As fast as the wind is,
As strong as the sea.
Lions are lovely!
They roar like a storm.
They run like a river.
They're soft and they're warm."

Tilly wanted to ride on her lion's back for ever and ever.

Suddenly, Lion stopped and put his head to one side, listening. He seemed to be able to hear something that Tilly couldn't hear. He pushed his head right into a low, dark bush, and then stepped back again.

Tilly slid off his back, and ran to see what he was doing. Hanging from Lion's mouth was a tiny kitten, as skinny as a bird.

"Oh, Lion, don't swallow it!" gasped Tilly.

Lion crouched down and gently dropped the kitten between his paws. The kitten lay there, quite still. Then Lion began to lick it, all over, under its stomach and round its ears and over its face, over and over, till at last the little kitten opened its eyes and tried to catch Lion's tongue in its paws. It wobbled onto its feet and then with its tiny tongue tried to lick Lion's enormous paws.

"Poor little thing," said Tilly. "What's it doing here, all on its own? Let's take it to Mrs Patel, Lion. She'll know what to do."

Mrs Patel's shop was at the corner of the park. She sold everything, including wonderful home-made jam and marmalade and cakes. Everybody came to Mrs Patel's shop.

Tilly climbed onto Lion's back, and Lion picked the kitten up in his huge mouth, and they sped across the park to the shop.

It was nearly closing time. Mrs Patel was outside her shop, painting the window ledge. She didn't seem at all surprised to see Lion when he pounded up to her, or to see Tilly on his back, or to see the kitten which Lion gently placed at her feet.

"What a lovely ginger kitten," she said. "He's the same colour as my marmalade."

"We found him in the park," said Tilly.

"He looks like a stray to me." Mrs Patel put down her brush and picked up the kitten. He was crying pitifully. "I wonder how he got here?"

"We brought him here!" said Tilly. The strange thing was that Mrs Patel didn't even look at her, or at Lion. She didn't really seem to *see* them.

"I'll give him some milk, and put him nice and warm in a box in the window, and see if anyone comes for him," said Mrs Patel, more to herself than to Tilly and Lion. She turned to go back into the shop.

"What if no one comes for him?" asked Tilly.

No. Mrs Patel hadn't seen her, or heard

her. As she opened the shop door to go in, Tilly could just hear her whispering to the kitten: "If nobody owns you, ginger kitten, I'll give you away." And she closed the door.

"Oh, Lion!" said Tilly.

Suddenly . . . *Ding-dong-ding-dong* . . . she heard the bells of the village church chime . . . *ding-dong-ding-dong* . . .

"Lion!" said Tilly. "It's six o'clock! Your programme will be finishing! What if it finishes without you? You might never get back to your jungle again! Oh, Lion, what will you do then? What will you do then?"

DONG! Lion stopped. He listened.

DONG! He tossed back his beautiful, bright head.

DONG! He turned; and faster than fishes, faster than lightning, faster than trains, he thundered back through the park to Tilly Mint's house.

DONG! Lion bounded up the street.

DONG! He leapt through Tilly's open window.

DONG! And on the sixth stroke of the church clock, he dived back through the television screen.

Tilly had slipped off his back, and onto her favourite soft-and-silky rug, which was as gold-and-red as any lion's head.

Lion's tail disappeared through the television screen just as the music came on for the end of the jungle film. Tilly heard him roar.

"Goodbye, lovely Lion!" Tilly called.

Mrs Hardcastle woke up with a jump. "Have I missed that programme?" she asked crossly. "That's the trouble with being as old as I am, Tilly Mint. I always fall asleep and miss things."

"You missed the lion, Mrs Hardcastle," Tilly said.

And then she said: "Mrs Hardcastle, when you were a little girl, years and years and years ago, and you saw a lion, did you ride on his back?"

"Yes," said Mrs Hardcastle, in a far-away remembery sort of voice. "I believe I did. It was lovely, Tilly Mint."

"Yes," said Tilly. "I know, Mrs Hardcastle. Lions are lovely. They're as gentle as milk."

And then she said, in her best voice, "By the way, Mrs Hardcastle, do you think Mum would let me have a kitten?"

"Ah," said Mrs Hardcastle. "Is it a ginger one?"

"Yes," said Tilly. "Like a jar of marmalade."

"Is it in Mrs Patel's shop?"

"Yes," said Tilly. "How do you know that?"

But Mrs Hardcastle only smiled her smile that knew everything.

"I'm sure your mum will let you have him," she said. "You could call him Lion."

And Tilly did.

Tilly Mint Sends
the Bird of Night Packing

On Saturday night, when the moon was as
bright as raindrops, and the stars were so
white that you'd think they were made of
ice, and the black between them was thick
enough to touch, Tilly Mint had the most
wonderful adventure of her life.

"That sky is just about prickling with
stars, Tilly Mint," Mrs Hardcastle said. "You
don't often see it like that. It's just the sort of
night you can hear the stars sing, if you listen
very carefully."

Tilly Mint listened very carefully, but all
she could hear was the old owl, hooting
away comfortably in his tree in the dark
wood.

"Old owl, cold owl, bird of light,
Tell your tale of stars tonight.
Old owl, cold owl, snowy-wing,
Take me to the stars that sing,"

said Mrs Hardcastle softly.

Tilly Mint shivered. How could the owl do that? How could she hear the stars sing?

"You're as cold as a goldfish, Tilly Mint!" said Mrs Hardcastle. "Pop into bed this minute, and I'll tell you about the time I heard the stars sing . . . many years ago."

But just as Tilly turned to hop into bed and just as Mrs Hardcastle started to draw the curtains, they heard a croaky cackle that made their bones creep.

"Caw!" it went. "Caw, caw, caw!"

"I don't like the sound of that!" said Mrs Hardcastle. Tilly had pulled her pillow over her head to keep the sound out.

"What is it, Mrs Hardcastle?"

"It sounded to me like the bird of night! I hope it wasn't . . ."

"Caw, caw," came the cackle again. "Caw . . ."

A black shadow filled the room.

"What was that?" asked Tilly.

"I don't like the look of that!" said Mrs Hardcastle. "It looked to me like the bird of night. I can't be sure. I've only see him once before, Tilly. He comes from long ago. But when he came, he put out all the stars. I've never seen blackness like it.

"Once, in the night, a black shadow flew.
In the deep darkness the shadow grew.
There was never a whisper; never a sigh,
From blackness to blackness it seemed to fly.
It wrapped the sky in its wings spread wide,
On the wind of a nightmare it seemed to ride;
And the moon and the stars all lost their light,
And the world was as black as the bird of
night."

"Can't we stop it?" cried Tilly Mint. "Can't anybody stop it?"

"The bird of light could help," Mrs Hardcastle said, "but he's very, very old. As old as me perhaps. The oldest woman in the world . . ." Mrs Hardcastle sat down beside Tilly's bed, closed her eyes, and began to snore, very gently. Mrs Hardcastle had gone to sleep.

Tilly saw the shadow again, and she heard that gritty grating noise that made her goose-pimples grow . . .

"Caw! Caw! Caw!"

She ran to the window, and she saw the huge bird of night, flapping up from the trees to the sky, spreading its massive wings till they covered the light of the moon and all

the stars. Never had Tilly seen such
blackness.

"Now I'll never hear the stars sing!" Tilly
shouted. "It's not fair!

And then, Tilly heard the owl.

"Hoo! Hoo-hoo! Hoooo!" Whiter than the
moon, and quieter than the night, the old
owl from the wood floated like a boat
towards her on the black sea of the sky.

"Owl!" said Tilly. "You've grown as big as
a swan! You're sailing in the sky like a swan
on a lake! Like a white ship! Where do you
think you're off to, as big as that?"

For an answer, the owl hooted again.
"Youoooooo! Come tooo! You. You. Come
toooooo!"

Tilly Mint remembered Mrs Hardcastle's
poem.

Old owl, cold owl, bird of light,
Tell your tale of stars tonight.
Old owl, cold owl, snowy-wing,
Take me to the stars that sing.

"Will you, oh, will you, Snowy-wing? Can
we chase away the bird of night?" Tilly asked.

The white owl drifted down till he was
just below Tilly's window. She put on her

fluffy slippers and her warm red dressing gown, and she opened her window and stepped out onto his back, onto the soft white feathers that snuggled round her like the soft, white cover of her bed. She put her arms round his neck, and she tucked her legs down beneath his wings.

"FLY! FLY!" said Tilly.

"Old owl, cold owl, bird of light,
Tell your tale of stars tonight.
Old owl, cold owl, snowy-wing,
Take me to the stars that sing,
Old owl, cold owl, white as light,
Chase away the bird of night!"

Up they flew, into the sky that was as black as the sea. Up they swam, in the thick waves of night. Up they sailed, in the dark, dark ocean of the sky. And, far away in the distance, they heard the angry, jangly call of the bird of night.

"Caw! Caw! Caw!"

Snowy-wing drove down his wings like oars, and skimmed higher and higher. The black bird of night flew away from him in rage.

"Go away, bird of night. Go home!"

shouted Tilly. "Clear off, you floppy old blanket!"

"Shooooooo! Shoooo! We don't want you!" called the owl.

And the black bird of night flew away, down, down, down, till his cross, crackling, croaky cry faded away and away and away. And was heard no more.

Then the moon came out again, and shone and sparkled as bright as raindrops. And the stars came, one by one, so white that you'd think they were made of ice. Tilly was right up with them; she heard them sing.

They sang from one end of the world to the other, and they sang like voices deep below the sea.

Much later, the white owl flew back down from the sky, with Tilly on his back.

She crept back in through the window, and snuggled into her bed, which was as white and soft as the feathers on the white owl's back.

Mrs Hardcastle woke up, and stretched. "I must have dropped off to sleep!" she said. "Good gracious, Tilly Mint, what are you doing, in bed with your dressing gown on?"

Tilly wriggled her feet. She still had her

slippers on, but she didn't say anything about that.

"Listen!" she said. "Listen, Mrs Hardcastle. You might just be able to hear the stars sing!"

Mrs Hardcastle listened very hard, but she was too old now, and much too far away, to hear the stars. All she could hear was the old white owl, hooting away comfortably in his tree in the dark, dark wood.

Tilly Mint Makes
a Frog-faced Friend

Mrs Hardcastle has a pond in her back garden. It's not very wide, and it's not very deep, but it has a sitting-stone at the side of it, like a little stool, and she sits there sometimes on nice days, nodding in the sunshine, and watching the fish. Sometimes, on *very* nice days, she takes her shoes off and sticks her feet in the water.

On the seventh of March she told Tilly that it was time to fetch some frog-spawn for the pond.

"I've never had a frog in my pond, Tilly," she said. "It would be nice, wouldn't it?"

"I don't think I've ever seen a frog," said Tilly. "Not a real one. I don't think I like them all that much."

"Not like frogs!" Mrs Hardcastle was astonished. "Good heavens, Tilly Mint. You like fish, don't you?"

"Yes, I think so."

"Well then. You'll like frogs. Bound to.

Come on, Tilly. Fetch a jam-jar, and we'll go frog-spawn hunting. And on the way home, we'll buy some fresh-baked bread and some strawberry jam for tea."

On the big pond in the park, ducks were quacking and turning upside down, and sticklebacks were zipping about, and little flies were dancing just above the water. The frog-spawn lay among the reeds, where the pond was shallow.

"Yuk!" said Tilly, in disgust. "Look at that! It's like jelly gone grey. It's like sago pudding in washing-up water."

"It's like little bubbles waiting to be popped," said Mrs Hardcastle. "Wait till these little black blobs turn into tadpoles, Tilly Mint. Wait till they grow their little tails, and swim round in my pond. Wait till they grow little legs, and crawl up onto our sitting-stone. Then you'll like them, when they're baby frogs."

"We'll just take a bit then," said Tilly, and she slid a blob of bubbly frog-spawn into a jar. "I shall probably like it a bit better, when it's a frog."

"Listen! Did you hear that?" said Mrs Hardcastle. "I'm sure I heard a frog croak just then."

"So did I," said Tilly. "But I can't see one, can you?"

They hunted round in the grass and under the stones and at the edge of the big pond, till Mrs Hardcastle was too tired to hunt any more. She sat down on a bench, and she closed her eyes, and she began to snore, very, very gently.

And then it was that Tilly heard the frog again.

"Croak, croak!"

And she saw it. It flopped across the grass towards her, and it was the colour of a leaf, or an apple, or the top of an onion, or a new lettuce. Tilly thought she had never seen anyone looking so sad.

"Frog," she croaked. "What's the matter?"

And this is the song the sad frog sang to her:

"I've lost my lovely frog-faced friend.
(Sigh with me. Come, cry with me.)
Without my love my days will end.
(Oh, come and croak with me.)
While others leap I watch and weep
On this cold stone I croak alone,
Who knows when my cracked heart will mend?
Oh, come and croak with me."

Frog croaked again, and Tilly croaked too.

Then Tilly picked up her jar of frog–spawn, and went over to where Mrs Hardcastle was snoring gently in the sunshine.

They walked back up the hill to Mrs Patel's shop, but Mrs Hardcastle was thoughtful, and Tilly was sad.

"It must be lonely, being a frog," said Tilly Mint at last.

"It is," said Mrs Hardcastle. "It's bad enough being an old lady."

They pushed open the shop door, and went into Mrs Patel's lovely, warm, appley–and–cheesy–and–new–baked–bread–smelling shop.

"Help yourselves!" sang out Mrs Patel, from the top of a ladder, and Mrs Hardcastle went to sniff the bread while Tilly chose the jam. She put her jar of frog-spawn on the shelf with the jars of jam, and thought how funny it would be if all the strawberries and raspberries and blackcurrants started bobbing round in their jars instead of lying all still and sticky in their ponds of jam, waiting to be eaten.

And then she thought of her sad frog again, sighing for his missing frog-faced friend. What could she do to help him?

What *could* she do to help him? She gazed
round Mrs Patel's shop, looking for a clue,
and it was then that she saw the messages on
the shop door. Envelopes, telling people about
things for sale, and things to buy, and things
that were lost, and things that were found.

FOR SALE, they said. BOY'S BIKE.

WANTED, they said. HUTCH FOR RABBIT.

LOST, they said. TABBY CAT. And FOUND.
ONE GLOVE.

That was it! She'd put a message for the
missing frog!

"Please, Mrs Hardcastle," she said, when
Mrs Hardcastle had paid for her bread and
nibbled the crusty bit off the end. "Can I put
a message on Mrs Patel's door? Can I put,
LOST, ONE FROG, just in case it happens to
pass by? Please?"

Well, Mrs Hardcastle wasn't sure that frogs
could read, and neither was Mrs Patel, but
they wrote the message out, just in case, and
stuck it on the door for everyone to read.
LOST, it said. ONE FROG. CONTACT TILLY MINT.

Tilly Mint and Mrs Hardcastle were nearly
at the top of the hill when Tilly remembered
the terrible thing she had done. She'd
forgotten! She forgotten the jar of frog-
spawn! She'd left it on the jam shelf in Mrs

Patel's shop!

Poor old Mrs Hardcastle was much too tired to go back down the hill again, so she sat on somebody's wall and had a little nap while Tilly charged down to the shop. She flung open the door and raced in. The shop doorbell jangled so loudly that Mrs Patel nearly fell off her ladder.

"Mrs Patel!" gasped Tilly. "You haven't sold my frog-spawn, have you?"

But she was quite safe. Nobody had taken it home for their tea. She lifted it carefully off the shelf, and as she was going out with it, Mrs Patel shouted: "By the way, Tilly. There's been an answer to your advert."

Sitting on the counter, looking very hopeful, was a green frog.

In great excitement, Tilly picked her up and carried her outside.

"Frog!" she croaked softly. "Have you lost your lovely frog-faced friend?"

Frog croaked.

"Hop down to the park," Tilly croaked. "And look on the stone by the bench by the pond. He's waiting for you there."

Frog flopped joyfully off towards the pond.

"And Frog!" Tilly called. "Come and see us at Mrs Hardcastle's pond, any time."

That night, after Tilly had emptied the frog-spawn from her jar into Mrs Hardcastle's pond, and after she'd had three slices of fresh crusty bread, sticky with fat strawberries for her tea, and after she'd said goodnight and gone to bed, she thought she heard the sound of a frog singing in the dark.

It might have been two frogs. It might have been coming from the sitting-stone at the side of the pond in Mrs Hardcastle's back garden.

"I hope it is," she said. And went to sleep.

"Deep in the green of the silent pond
Where fingers of fern reach out to the light;

The cold fins glitter,
The pale eye gleams,
The ghost-fish flicker and drift like dreams:
And in the cool moonlight, dark in the
     dead-night,
The voice of the frog is heard in the land."

The Island of Dreams

"What shall we do today, Tilly Mint?" asked Mrs Hardcastle, when Tilly knocked at her door. "Shall we go to the shops, or make some buns, or do you want to pop down with me to the Island of Dreams?"

"What!" said Tilly. "We're always going to the shops. And we're always making buns. But I've never even *heard* of the Island of Dreams. What are we waiting for?"

She ran round, looking for the bits and pieces that Mrs Hardcastle could never find, like her shoes, and her handbag, and her key, and her headscarf. She tied her shoelaces for her, and she gave her a digestive biscuit to stop her tummy rumbling, and they were off: running down the hill and over the road to the park.

They leaned against a tree, panting, to get their breath back.

"Well," said Tilly. "Where is this island, Mrs Hardcastle?"

72

Mrs Hardcastle looked round, a bit worried.

"That's just it," she said. "I can't remember. It's years and years since I went there. But it's round here somewhere, I'm sure of it."

They looked round a bit more, and then Mrs Hardcastle said, "I remember, Tilly. We have to get there by boat!"

They climbed into one of the green boats that were tied up at the side of the lake ready for the summer.

"You'll have to help me to row, Tilly," said Mrs Hardcastle. "My arms aren't as rubbery as they used to be."

Seven ducks lined up behind them, and three swans floated in front. Tilly and Mrs Hardcastle took an oar each. And they rowed.

Tilly loved the sound the oars made. It made her think of shiny, fat fish, leaping up out of the water. She loved the up-and-down rocking of the boat. And she loved the sound of the ducks quacking round them, tipping up their tails in the water, quacking and quacking as if the little green boat was one of them.

And as they rowed, and as they quacked,

Mrs Hardcastle sang at the top of her voice. Only it wasn't really a song. It sounded a bit like a shopping list. It sounded a bit like a recipe for something new to bake.

"Petals and cobwebs and butterfly wings,
Ground to a powder, mix it and mingle it.
Soak it in dewdrops and summer-breeze dry it.
Feather-light float it in cool of the moonlight.
Fill it with shadows of goblins and dragons
And whispers of fairies and harebells and bees.
Colour it rainbow and wrap it in snowflakes
And drink it at sleep-time to sweeten your
dreams.

"Don't forget the dream-dust, will you, Tilly Mint?" she said. "I'm right out of it. That's what we've come for, if we ever find the place."

Tilly was too excited to speak.

Mrs Hardcastle stood up in the boat so suddenly that she nearly flipped right out of it into the water. "There it is!" she said. "There's the Island of Dreams."

A mist lay across the water in front of them, so low and so thick that nothing could be seen. And as they sailed into it, it swallowed all the sound up, so nothing could be heard.

The singing, and the rowing and the
quacking all stopped, and they floated towards
a large rock, and deep into a hole that was as
black as a wide toothless mouth. They were in
a cave, with water drip-drip-dripping all
around them.

"I don't like it, Mrs Hardcastle," Tilly
whispered. "Let's go home and bake buns."

But Mrs Hardcastle said, "Tilly Mint, don't
you ever let me find you trying to run away
from magic."

Magic!

"Pop out and fetch me some dream-dust,
there's a good girl," said Mrs Hardcastle. "I'm
so tired." She yawned dozily. "That's the
trouble with being the oldest woman in the
world – can't seem to sleep without dream-
dust these days. Petals . . . and cobwebs . . .
and butterfly wings. Remember that, Tilly
Mint."

Before Tilly had time to ask her how many,
and where from, and how, Mrs Hardcastle had
closed her eyes, and opened her mouth, and
was snoring, very, very gently.

"Well," said Tilly to herself, thinking that
Mrs Hardcastle was hardly ever awake these
days. "Now what do I do?" And the only
answer was the echo of her own voice, round

and round in the cold, dark cave. "Now what do I do? Do I do? Do? Do?"

Then she saw hundreds of tiny lights dancing round her, and she felt hundreds of tiny hands clutching at her own. She stood up, and the tiny hands pulled her and pushed her till she was whizzing, faster and faster, on the slippiest helter-skelter of her life. Wheeeee! Right into a fairground.

In front of her was a merry-go-round of shiny red and black and grey horses. Tilly was so excited that she completely forgot what she'd come for. She climbed on the back of the nearest merry-go-round horse – the red one – and they were off!

But this horse didn't go up and down. This horse didn't go round and round. It galloped, red as a poppy; it galloped away from the fairground and into a forest that was strewn with petals and dangling with cobwebs and dancing with butterflies. Its black hooves thundered on the grass and sent up dazzling showers of dewdrops.

"I'm wet!" shouted Tilly. "Red horse! I'm wet through!" But a breeze that was as soft and warm as a summer's day dried her.

The red horse galloped through the forest

till it came to a cliff, and without even pausing to look down, it galloped over the edge and into the air and floated, slow as a feather, in the silver light of the moon.

Tilly clung to it and laughed with joy. Black shapes flickered and flitted round her, calling and cackling, goblin-shaped, with bent backs and bony fingers; and dragon-shaped, with red breath as hot as a kettle, but they didn't worry Tilly. All round her she could hear the whisper of fairies, and the chiming of harebells, and the lovely buzz of bees. She knew she was safe.

Then, all of a sudden, it began to snow. Every snowflake had the colours of a rainbow hidden in the heart of it. Tilly opened her mouth to catch them, and they tasted as feathery-fizzy as sherbet. Snowflakes settled in her hair, on her eyelids, on her tongue. They covered her red horse.

The horse galloped down from the air onto the land. A hundred dancing lights led them down a steep path to the edge of the water. Hundreds of tiny hands helped Tilly to climb down from the horse.

"Goodbye, red horse," she called. "Goodbye!"

The red horse stamped its hoof and

whinnied. "Goodbye," it seemed to say, and galloped away into the mist.

Tilly Mint heard a snore, and a whistle, and she turned round to see the little green boat bobbing on the black water of the cave, and Mrs Hardcastle just beginning to wake up. And then she remembered. The dream—dust! She'd forgotten all about it.

"What shall I do?" she whispered. And the echo of the cave answered, "What shall I do? Shall I do? Do? Do?"

Tilly climbed into the boat, still wondering what she could say to Mrs Hardcastle.

"Have you had a lovely time?" Mrs Hardcastle asked.

"Yes," said Tilly. "Yes. But you see . . ."

"And just look at all that dream-dust you've brought back!" said Mrs Hardcastle. "You look like a sparkler, Tilly Mint. You're covered in it."

And so she was. Just like her red horse, she was covered in a fine dust of gold and silver. It probably went all down her tummy too. Mrs Hardcastle opened her handbag, and brushed all Tilly's dream-dust into it, and closed it up tight.

"Let's go home for tea now, shall we?" she said.

And they did. But when they looked back

from the park to the lake, it was as blue as blue. No rock. No mist. The Island of Dreams had disappeared — just as if it had never been there at all.

Goodbye, Mrs Hardcastle

This morning, as soon as Tilly woke up, she knew it was going to be a very special day. One of those days when there's no point in staying in bed. The sunlight pushed its way through the curtains like marmalade oozing between two slices of bread. Tilly could hear the birds shouting.

And somebody was banging stones about.

She opened her bedroom window and saw, a few gardens down, Mrs Hardcastle, still in her dressing gown and slippers. She seemed to be poking under things, and turning things over, and tapping on things.

"Have you lost something, Mrs Hardcastle?" Tilly shouted.

Mrs Hardcastle waved to her. "Lost something? No, I'm waking things up, Tilly. I want to have a party!"

Tilly drew her head back in, pulled on her dressing gown and slippers, and ran out of the bedroom. Mum caught her as she was running past the door.

"Just a minute, Tilly Mint," she said. "What's all that noise about, this time of the morning?"

"It's Mrs Hardcastle," said Tilly.

"I might have known," said Mum. "Does she realize it's not six o'clock yet?"

"She's waking things up," Tilly explained.

A noise like a parade bugled across the gardens.

"She's blowing a trumpet!" said Mum. "Will you just listen to her!"

They ran back into Tilly's room and poked their heads through the top of the window again. And they weren't the only ones. All along the street, curtains were being pulled back and windows were being opened and white, morning, yawning faces, some of them with no teeth in their mouths, and some of them with rollers in their hair, and all of them cross with not enough sleep anyway, poked out. Birds stood open-beaked on their branches. Hedgehogs and tortoises stood stock-still. All the flowers opened at once.

Mrs Hardcastle put her trumpet down and beamed up at the windows.

"Good morning, everyone!" she said.

"Good morning, Mrs Hardcastle," said Tilly.

"It's my birthday," said Mrs Hardcastle.

"Hurray!" said Tilly.

"And you're all invited to my party."

"Where?" said Tilly. "When?"

"Now. In the park."

All the windows closed at once. Tilly put
on her green dungarees and her stripy blue-
and-white shirt, and Mum put on her red
smock and her blue jeans, and they ran
down to the park.

As they ran, they were joined by all Tilly's
friends and Mrs Patel from the shop; and
some people on their way to work, like
postmen and milkmen; and some people on
their way home from work, like nurses and
factory workers, and they all changed their
minds about going to work or to bed and
went off down to the park instead.

Dawn was still pink in the sky, and the
early morning mist was still grey on the grass.
Surprised spiders scrambled up their cobwebs
as all those feet scurried past. Ducks flew up
from the pond in amazement. Delighted frogs
croaked.

Mrs Hardcastle had brought down a basket
of cooked sausages and another basket of
bread, and everyone helped themselves.

Then you should have seen how all the
people danced, round the lake, up and down

the river banks, in and out of the trees.

Mrs Hardcastle was sitting on a bench, watching them all and blowing up dozens of balloons.

"Mrs Hardcastle," whispered Tilly. "How about showing them some magic?"

"What!" said Mrs Hardcastle.

"As it's a very special day?" pleaded Tilly. "Go on. I just feel like a bit of magic!"

Mrs Hardcastle went on blowing up balloons. "I'm the oldest woman in the world, Tilly Mint," she sighed. "Even older, now it's my birthday. And the longer I've lived, and the older I've grown, the more I've found out that only very special people can see magic when it happens. Or hear it. Or feel it. It's there all the time, and nobody even notices.

"Nobody notices magic things,
Nobody sees, and nobody hears.
Nobody knows when the magic's there,
Nobody, nobody cares."

She blew her nose, very loudly, on her handkerchief.

"But I do!" said Tilly. "I notice! I care! Couldn't we just try them?"

Mrs Hardcastle gave Tilly some of the

balloons, and they went round together to hand them round to everybody.

What a lot of pushing there was! A brother and sister who lived in Tilly's street started fighting each other because they both wanted the same balloon.

"Careful!" said Tilly. "These are magic balloons, you know!"

"Magic!" the brother and sister laughed. "There's no such thing!" But their balloon popped, and they didn't get another one.

"Now!" said Mrs Hardcastle at last. "We're ready."

She blew her trumpet again, and everyone gathered round them. She and Tilly stood in the middle, just near where Tilly had seen the leaf-lords dance, all that time ago. Everybody held up their arms, so the balloons danced on their strings above their heads; blue, yellow, green, red, orange, pink and white. They danced and they danced and they danced.

"When the wind whispers,
When the rain calls,
When the moon winks,
And tiny stars fall,
When the earth breathes,
When the sea sighs,

It's time for the magic
To kiss your eyes . . ."

"I know what's going to happen now," said Tilly. "You're going to start snoring, so the magic can come."

"Oh no, I'm not, Tilly Mint," said Mrs Hardcastle. "I'm sick of missing all the fun. I'm going up! Wheee!"

And up she went, clutching her red balloon high above her head.

"Come on, Tilly!" she shouted.

"This is great. I haven't done this for years!"

Tilly felt the string of her balloon tugging, and her feet lifting off the ground, and up she went after Mrs Hardcastle. Wheee!

"Come on, everybody!" she called down to all the faces turned up like daisies to watch. "You can come too!"

Some of Tilly's friends started floating up straight away, but their mothers caught them by the feet and dragged them down again. Some people thought they would float higher if they jumped off trees, but their balloons popped in the branches as they tried to climb up. Some people were frightened when they felt their balloons lifting them up, and they let go of the strings. Away their balloons floated, up to the clouds.

Tilly's mum and Mrs Patel and all Mrs Patel's children bobbed up, and then down again, and up again, and down. They couldn't believe what was happening to them!

So, in the end, there were only Tilly and Mrs Hardcastle in the sky, floating over the park. Far below them, all the people were waving.

Tilly felt as if she was dancing in the blue sky. She felt she could dance for ever, holding on to her balloon that was as yellow as the sun.

Mrs Hardcastle bobbed over to her. "Time

to go down now, Tilly Mint," she said. And then she said, "I've got something for you in my handbag. Here it is, Tilly. Take care of it."

"But, Mrs Hardcastle," Tilly gasped.

"Goodbye, Tilly," Mrs Hardcastle said.

"But, Mrs Hardcastle. Aren't you coming down with me?" Tilly was already floating down, and Mrs Hardcastle was already floating up.

"Goodbye, Tilly," Mrs Hardcastle called, in a far-away voice. "I want to go on flying now. I'm having an adventure, Tilly Mint. I've been wanting to do this since long, long ago . . ."

Her voice grew fainter and fainter, and suddenly there was a bump, and Tilly was lying on the grass in the park. Mum was sitting on a bench nearby, reading the paper.

"Hello," said Mum. "What have you got there, Tilly Mint?"

"It's a handbag," said Tilly. She opened it up carefully, keeping the sparkle in. "It's full of dream-dust."

Tilly looked up at the sky. She could just see a brown blob that could have been a skylark, and a blue thing that could have been a butterfly, and a tiny red bobbing thing that could have been a bubble. But Tilly knew what it was.

"Bye, Mrs Hardcastle," she whispered.

And Tilly Mint and Mum walked back home for lunch.

TILLY MINT
AND THE DODO

In loving memory of the last dodo, which
was killled by pirates on the island of
Mauritius in 1681, and in honour of all
extinct and endangered species.

Chapter One

A Message from Mrs Hardcastle

It was a very windy night; the sort of night that sounds as if wild animals are roaring round the house, and pawing at the door to be let in. The sort of night that looks as if the stars are the eyes of those animals, cold and angry.

Tilly Mint couldn't sleep. She snuggled under her quilt to try and block the noise out, but still the wild animals of the wind howled at her, and still the eyes of the stars glared down at her.

"Something nice will happen," she told herself. "And then I'll be able to go to sleep."

The animals in the wind laughed.

"Yes it will," said Tilly. "I know it will."

The big eye of the moon winked at her as it slid away from the clouds. Through her window Tilly could see the leaves being torn from trees, and twigs and branches too, as if they were alive and rushing for shelter. Then she saw something long and blue twisting about like an eel; wrapping itself round things and tearing itself free; dancing, as if it didn't care about the wind.

"I've seen that before," said Tilly Mint to herself. "I know I have."

And then she saw something round and red, cheerful as summer, bobbing like a bubble, and she knew she'd seen that before too. She pressed her face to the window to see what else was there, and soon there came another shape, darker than the red one, and much rounder, and quite a bit bigger, and hanging onto it by a piece of string: a Mrs Hardcastle sort of shape. Tilly sat back on her heels, not daring to believe what she'd seen.

"It can't be," she said, though she knew it was. She pulled Mr Pig out from under her pillow and held him up to have a look too.

"Look, Mr Pig," she whispered. "You know who that is, don't you? It's Mrs Hardcastle! Everybody said she'd gone away for ever, but I knew I'd see her again!"

Tilly Mint missed Mrs Hardcastle very much. Everybody said that she'd never see her again, but Tilly knew, in her heart of hearts, that somebody as magic as Mrs Hardcastle couldn't possibly stay away for ever.

But when she looked again the red thing,

and the blue thing, and the darker thing had all gone. The moon had slipped like a fox back down into the dark clouds, and the animal stars had closed their staring eyes. The wind had stopped its roaring and was just sighing gently, like someone in a deep sleep. Tilly pushed Mr Pig back under her pillow, where she knew he'd be warm, and she wriggled back under her quilt again.

"I knew something nice was going to happen," she said.

Just as Tilly was drifting into sleep the red thing and the blue thing and the darker thing landed with a gentle bump in the middle of the woods at the end of the park that was just down the road from Tilly Mint's house. The darker thing, Mrs Hardcastle, stood up carefully. She was a bit stiff after her long flight. She tied her red balloon to an overhanging branch, and then she climbed up the tree a bit to rescue her tangled blue scarf.

"What a mess this place is in," she said to herself, looking round. "No animals to be seen. All the flowers squashed. Someone's been chopping trees down. And all the birds are hiding! Something had better be done

about all this before it's too late. I think I
know just the right person to help me, too."

Next morning there was a letter for Tilly
under the milk bottle on the step. Tilly wasn't
a bit surprised to see it, though her mum was.

Dear Tilly Mint I'm having a little
holiday in my cottage in the country. Can
you bring me the box of special things I left
in my attic? I've got an important job for you
to do. Love, Mrs. Hardcastle.

She read her letter again and again. The
strange thing was, Mum was quite sure that
Tilly Mint had written the letter herself, and
if you looked at it closely you could see that
the writing was very like Tilly's, a bit scrawly,
and a bit splodgy. You could even tell where
she'd had to rub things out because she'd
made spelling mistakes. But of course, as Tilly
Mint pointed out, she couldn't possibly have
written it herself. She'd been fast asleep all
night.

"And I saw Mrs Hardcastle flying past,"
she said.

Mum smiled and told her to eat up
her breakfast, and Tilly slid her letter under
her plate and read it every time Mum

wasn't looking.

"Dear Tilly Mint, I'm having a little holiday in my cottage in the country. Can you bring me the box of special things I left in my attic? I've got an important job for you to do. Love, Mrs Hardcastle."

I wonder where Mrs Hardcastle's country cottage could be, thought Tilly. And what kind of special things could Mrs Hardcastle have left in her attic? And my job! What's my important job going to be?

Tilly knew that she couldn't be bothered to finish her toast, even though it was sticky with the yellow marmalade that she'd helped to make. She didn't even want any more orange juice to drink. She was definitely too excited to help to clear the table.

"Can I go?" she begged. "Please, please, Mum? Can I go round to see Captain Cloud?"

And at last Mum said yes, and Tilly Mint ran like last night's wind to the house where Mrs Hardcastle used to live, and where Captain Cloud lived now.

Tilly would never forget the day Captain Cloud had arrived in her street. He hadn't just walked along the pavement as anyone else would have done. He'd come by boat!

On the rainiest day Tilly Mint had ever known Captain Cloud had rowed up the street in a little green boat and parked it outside Mrs Hardcastle's house. Tilly was the only one who'd seen him do that. Everyone knew that he was Mrs Hardcastle's brother, and that he'd come to stay. Every time it rains he brings his boat out and rows up and down the street in it, just for fun, when Tilly's the only one looking.

If you've ever seen Captain Cloud, you'll know what he looks like. His face is as brown as a nutmeg, and his beard is as grey as clouds on a rainy day. He wears huge green wellies that come right up to his armpits, as if he's been poured into them, and his pockets are full of shells, and he smells of the tide when it's full of fish.

When Tilly knocked on the door, Captain Cloud was in his kitchen, singing a song about a jellyfish . . .

"*Proper little squelchy things*
Blobs of slime
Pink and purple bubbles
Dancers in the brine
Swirling out their skirtses
Watch them do their curtsies

Swaying in the waves like washing on the line . . ."

"Captain Cloud!" Tilly shouted through his letter box. "Can I come in, please?"

"Why, it's Tadpole Tilly! Pleased to see you," Captain Cloud shouted through the other side of the letter box. "Come on in, little shrimp! You're just in time to hear my new song!"

"I heard it," said Tilly. "It was good."

"Thank you. Very kind of you to say so. Would you like to hear it again?"

"Please let me come in, Captain Cloud! I've had a message from Mrs Hardcastle, and it's important."

Captain Cloud was as excited as Tilly was when he saw the letter.

"Country cottage, eh?" he said, stroking his cloud-wisp beard. "Important job, eh? Wonder what that can be? Special things! In the attic! Well, I'll be barnacled!"

"Please, Captain Cloud, can we go and look?"

Tilly ran up the stairs with Captain Cloud puffing behind her. They went right up to the very top of the house, to the dark and spidery attic where Mrs Hardcastle used to keep her

most special things; the precious things that
had belonged to her when she was a little
girl, years and years and years ago.

"Oh, Captain Cloud," whispered Tilly.
"Isn't it lovely in here!"

It was a most wonderful attic, dim and
quiet as a bat's cave, and draped with
fluttering scarves and long birds' feathers, and
piled with shells that had the sound of the sea
in them, and pebbles the colour of rivers, and
stones with fossils curled inside. And in the
corner, lit by the dusty light from the
cobwebby window, was an old basket with a
piece of paper tied to the handle.

SPECIAL THINGS, the label said. CARE OF
TILLY MINT.

"Captain Cloud, I've found it!" said Tilly.
She pulled back the dusty headscarf that was
covering the contents of the basket and
peered in.

"There's a long black shiny thing," she
said. "But I don't know what it is."

"Let's have a look," said Captain Cloud.
"Why, that's a spyglass, Tilly-turnip-head!
You look through it and you see things. You
spy on things, Tilly!"

Captain Cloud crawled round the attic,
spying on spiders and moths and blue bottles,

while Tilly brought the other special things out of Mrs Hardcastle's basket.

"There's a yellow balloon," she said. "Waiting to be blown up. And a little blue feather. Haven't I seen this before? And there's a drawing of a funny-looking bird. I think Mrs Hardcastle must have been trying to draw a turkey, and it's gone wrong. Oh, and look, Captain Cloud. Look!"

At the bottom of the basket, wrapped up in one of Mrs Hardcastle's orange dusters, was an egg. It was as big as a melon, and it was pale gold. They looked at it through the spyglass, and they polished it with the duster, and they held it up to the light of the window, and, very gently, they put it back in the basket.

"What is it, Captain Cloud?" asked Tilly.

"I don't know," he said. "I've never seen anything like that before. Never, never, in all my travels. It looks very special to me, Tilly Mint. I'll tell you something; it looks important, but I'm blowed if I know why."

He looked down at it again and scratched his cottony hair under his cap, and then he lifted up the basket and hooked it over Tilly's arm. 'If I were you I'd set off straight away with it and take it to Mrs Hardcastle."

"That's just the trouble." Tilly followed him down the stairs to his salty kitchen. "I don't really know where she is. I don't know how to find her. And look, Captain Cloud. It's raining!"

He came over to the window and stood looking out at the grey drizzle splattering down the glass. He loved the rain. It was his favourite weather. He once told Tilly that when it rained anything could happen. Anything . . .

"Why, little Tilly Lobster, you don't have to let that bother you!" he said, and his voice was bubbly with excitement. "Rain is just what you need!"

"Is it? I don't think I'll get very far in the rain, Captain Cloud."

"I'd say rain is just right." He opened the door. "Bring the basket!"

Tilly followed him down the path to the shed at the bottom of his garden. She had to duck between the raindrops, they were so fat. They slid between the cracks on the path and tumbled against each other. By the time Tilly had caught up with Captain Cloud a little river of rain was nibbling round her ankles.

"I don't like this much," she said.

"Yes you do," said Captain Cloud. "Look."

He opened up his shed door. "Just right!" he breathed. The floor had turned into a pool of browny-green water that slapped against the wooden walls. And bobbing against the side, moored to a hosepipe, was his green boat.

"In you get, Tiddlywink!"

Captain Cloud hauled the boat in and lifted Tilly and her basket onto the slippery seat.

"What's happening?" asked Tilly.

"Nothing much," said Captain Cloud. "Not to me, anyway. I'm going to polish my goldfish bowl today, that's what I'm going to do. But you, Tilly Fish, you are going to find Mrs Hardcastle."

He poked his head out of the shed to look at the weather. Tilly could hear the rain gushing down the path now, like a river rushing to the sea.

"This should do it," Captain Cloud said. "Hold on tight as a barnacle, Tilly-my-lizard. I'm going to give you a push."

Before Tilly knew what was happening, Captain Cloud had pushed the little boat out of the shed into the garden that was shimmering like a lake, and away she sailed;

away from the shed, away from the house, away from all the houses in her street, and far, far away from Captain Cloud in his long green wellie legs, waving to her from the door of his boat shed.

"Bye, Skipper Mint!" he called. "Give my love to Mrs Hardcastle!"

"Bye!" Tilly shouted back. She closed her eyes and let herself be rocked backwards and forwards in the little bobbing boat.

"Soon," she whispered. "Soon, I'll see Mrs Hardcastle again."

And, because the rocking of the boat made her very tired, she fell asleep.

Chapter Two

The Hideaway Woods

Tilly was woken up by the sound of knocking. Her boat was bumping gently against the roots of a tree. She lifted her basket out and then clambered up onto a reedy bank, tying the boat to a twisty root that stuck out like an elbow over the water.

There was no sign of a cottage anywhere, but when she bent down to pick up her basket, she noticed a crowd of mushrooms all huddled together like little bald men at a party. They were growing in the shape of an arrow, and pointing into the woods. She followed the arrow, and there was another, and another, all gleaming in the dark undergrowth.

"I hope this is the right way," Tilly said.

A rabbit came quietly along the path towards her.

"Is this the way to Mrs Hardcastle's?" Tilly asked it, and the rabbit turned and scampered off, flashing its tail like a torch for her to follow.

"This way! This way!" the birds in the trees sang down to her.

Tilly started to run, excited because she knew she must be nearly there now. Whiskers peeped out of holes, and paws stretched out to pull back brambles for her, and there, at last, she came to the biggest tree in the woods, a huge old chestnut tree with flowers like Christmas candles on its branches, and hanging down from it was a painted sign:

WELCOME, it said. MRS HARDCASTLE'S COUNTRY COTTAGE.

"Mrs Hardcastle! I'm here! I'm here!" Tilly shouted, running round the tree and looking up as if she expected to find Mrs Hardcastle sitting up in the branches with her legs dangling down. "I'm here!"

Then she noticed a shiny brown conker hanging on a piece of string from a twig. She reached up and pulled it, and from somewhere deep inside the tree came the sound of a bell ringing. The tree creaked, and a door slowly opened. Tilly crouched down to crawl in, and found herself face to face with a badger.

"Hello!" she said. "I've come to see Mrs Hardcastle."

The stripes on Badger's face were white with surprise. He snuffled up to Tilly to get a better smell of her.

"Just a minute," he grunted. He turned round and spoke anxiously into the darkness inside the tree.

"It's a person," he muttered. "And it wants to come in."

"Mrs Hardcastle, it's me!" Tilly shouted over his shoulder. "It's Tilly Mint!"

"Let her in, Badger!" sang out Mrs Hardcastle. "Tilly's our special friend."

Badger's face crumpled into smiles of welcome. He pulled open the door for Tilly to crawl in past him. And when she stood up, there was Mrs Hardcastle, smiling at her as if she'd never been away, sitting round the table having tea with her friends.

Tilly gazed about her. She didn't know where to look first.

She was standing inside a round wooden room, with just a flicker of daylight filtering through the chimney at the top. The walls of the room were knobbly and mossy. Long curtains of trailing green and brown leaves swayed over the window holes, casting dancing speckles of sunlight and shadows.

In the middle of the tree-room was a ring

of stones, with a small fire of twigs and nutshells crackling inside it, and on top of that, a kettle steaming for tea. There was a rocking chair made of bendy branches, with grass and leaves piled on it for a cushion, and a bed made of downy birds' feathers. The floor of the tree-room was sprinkled with soft pine needles that had melted down into a fine dust. The scent of these needles mingled with the sharp smell of the woodsmoke and with the rich deep breath of mushrooms and foxes and earth. Tilly breathed it in slowly, loving it.

"Mmm! Lovely!" she said.

"It is, isn't it," agreed Mrs Hardcastle. "Much nicer than most houses. Come and sit down and have some tea, Tilly. Come and meet my friends."

Badger, who seemed to be a bit slow and lame, hobbled over to the table with a tree stump for Tilly to sit on.

"We're so pleased you've come at last!" he kept chuckling. "We've been waiting and waiting."

A small rabbit was sitting next to Mrs Hardcastle and nibbling away fiercely at a lettuce. He watched nervously as Tilly pulled up her stump and sat next to him.

"You promise you won't start chasing us or

anything, will you?" he asked her.

"Now, Rabbit, I told you, didn't I?" Mrs Hardcastle said. "You can trust Tilly."

"Don't trust anyone, that's my motto," the rabbit said. "Especially humans." He said this softly, but Mrs Hardcastle heard him all right. She frowned at him, and he sighed and tore off a lettuce leaf with his teeth and offered it to Tilly. She noticed then that he had one arm tied up in a sling.

A hedgehog with a badly bruised face lapped slowly at a saucer of milk, and its babies snuffled round it, glinting timidly up at Tilly. A mouse with both its legs bandaged up rolled some seeds across the table for Tilly to chew. They tasted quite good.

"Are they all hurt?" Tilly whispered.

Mrs Hardcastle nodded. "I found most of them in traps and snares, Tilly, though Hedgehog here had walked into a car. They're all a bit nervous of humans, as you can see. But I've told them all that you're coming to help, and they've been looking forward to meeting you. Haven't you?"

Her animal friends all nodded enthusiastically. Even Rabbit managed a toothy grin, after Tilly had stroked him behind the ears.

"But what are they all doing here, Mrs Hardcastle, in this tree house?"

"Have an apple, and I'll tell you all about them. You're in the Hideaway Woods, by the way. Some of the most special creatures in the world live here."

She took two apples out of the pocket of her pinny and handed one to Tilly. They were the noisy sort that scrunch when you eat them, the juicy sort that trickle down your chin when you bite into them, the sort that smell so sharp and sweet that they make your throat ache to think about them.

"We've got a lot to do," said Mrs Hardcastle, when she'd crunched through the first half of her apple. "You've got to help me save a lot of birds and flowers and animals that are in terrible danger. Will you help me, Tilly Mint?"

Tilly sucked her apple core.

"What do you want me to do, Mrs Hardcastle?"

"I want you to listen to a very sad story, and then I want you to tell that story to every child you meet. Every single child. Will you promise me that?"

Tilly nodded. Above her head a family of bats were hanging upside down like a row of folded black umbrellas in their nursery roost. One of them shifted its raggedy tattered glove of a wing and peeped down at Tilly; a little mouse-face, dark and fuzzy as a bee, blinking with sleepy surprise; then it tugged its head in again and went back to sleep.

"Those are special bats," said Mrs Hardcastle. "They've been in terrible danger, Tilly, and there's not many of them left. But they're quite safe here, while I'm minding them."

As Tilly watched them she felt something watching her. A creamy-backed barn owl swooped down from the high lip of the tree's opening to stare at her.

"Quite safe," Mrs Hardcastle told her. "You're quite safe with Tilly Mint. She's my friend, too. Now, Tilly, have you brought me the things I sent for?"

"The special things from your attic? Yes, I have."

Tilly bent down to pick up the basket from the floor, and realized that there was an acorn-cup balanced on the edge of the stump next to hers, with a water-beetle floating on it. The water-beetle peered up at Tilly then nose-dived down out of sight. The tree stump was hollowed out and filled with rainwater.

There were two bubbles in it, and as she watched one of the bubbles winked at her, and then the other.

"They're eyes!" gasped Tilly. "Mrs Hardcastle, there's somebody in this tree stump!"

"That's Natterjack!" Mrs Hardcastle laughed. "Hop out, Natterjack, and say hello to Tilly."

A small toad hopped onto the side of the stump and blinked at Tilly with its jewel eyes.

"You look a bit fed up," said Tilly.

"You'd be fed up if you were me," Natterjack croaked. "I've lost my pond. I only hopped away for a couple of days, and when I went back someone had filled it up with stones and soil. All the water had gone!"

"But you're very welcome here," Mrs Hardcastle reminded him. "Till we find another pond for you and Beetle."

Natterjack bulged his throat out and made a sigh that sounded like a balloon going down. "It's not the same thing, Mrs Hardcastle. Not the same thing at all."

He kicked his back legs out and flopped into his tree-stump pond, till all they could see of him was the top of his head and his bubble eyes staring.

"Let's have the basket, Tilly!" Mrs Hardcastle laughed. "What did you bring me?"

The animals at the table crowded round Tilly to see what she'd brought. The mouse with the bandaged legs managed to clamber up the side of the basket and then fell in, and lay there with his legs in the air, stuck.

"Serves you right for being nosy, Mouse!" Mrs Hardcastle told him, but she lifted him out gently and set him back on his tree stump.

Tilly lifted out the spyglass first.

"My spyglass! Oh, hand it over!" Mrs Hardcastle stood up and screwed up her eye as she held the spyglass to it. "The things I can see through here! I can keep an eye on all my animals now. I can see newts and tigers and golden eagles and brown moths! I can see backwards and forwards in time, and up mountains and down caves, and round all the corners of the world. And I can see a special island, Tilly, far away. Look!"

She handed the spyglass to Tilly, but all she could see was a fuzzy ring with something green in the middle.

"What else have you brought?" asked Mrs Hardcastle.

Tilly dipped into the basket again. "I've brought your balloon, Mrs Hardcastle. Are we going to have a party?"

Mrs Hardcastle looked puzzled. "Party? No, I don't think so. I can't remember why I asked you to bring the balloon now. Never mind. I'm sure it'll come in useful. Anything else?"

"A feather."

"A feather! How strange! It's a very nice feather though, isn't it? It reminds me of a friend of mine."

"Mr Feathers!" Now Tilly remembered where she'd seen it before: at the bottom of the budgie cage that Mrs Hardcastle used to have in her kitchen.

"How is Mr Feathers, Tilly?"

"He flew away, Mrs Hardcastle. Just like you did."

"Did he now!" Mrs Hardcastle looked surprised, and then she smiled. "Good for him. Best thing a bird can do, to fly away. Hope he's all right though. Anything else?"

"A drawing. I think it's supposed to be a turkey, but you've got the neck all wrong. If you've got any felt pens I can show you how to get it right . . ."

Mrs Hardcastle snatched the drawing out

of her hands. Tilly sat very still, and a bit worried, thinking that she'd hurt Mrs Hardcastle's feelings. "Actually, it's quite a good turkey," she said. "I like its legs."

"This isn't a turkey, Tilly Mint. This is a dodo. Don't you know a dodo when you see one?"

Tilly peered at the drawing. She was sure she'd never seen a bird quite like that before – very plump, with little yellow legs and a clumpy crooked beak.

"No, Mrs Hardcastle. I don't think so. What is a dodo?"

Mrs Hardcastle sighed. "Dodos are like dinosaurs. They're all dead now." And she said it as if she was talking about some of her best friends. "A bit like turkeys, too. Big, fat birds. And they're a bit like you, really. They don't know how to fly. But the most important thing about them is that they've all gone, Tilly. They're all dead. No one will ever see a dodo again. Ever."

"Why, Mrs Hardcastle? Why did they all die?"

"Well, it's a long story. And it all happened a long time ago. I'll tell you later how it happened. You'll see."

Tilly could tell that Mrs Hardcastle didn't

really want to talk about it just now. "Poor dodos," she said.

"Yes, poor dodos. They never did anyone any harm."

"Mrs Hardcastle," said Tilly, after they had both sat quiet and thinking for a while. "When you were a little girl, years and years and years ago, did you ever see a dodo?"

"I'm not going to tell you, Tilly Mint! What a question! It's over three hundred years since anyone saw a dodo! You'll be asking me if I remember the dinosaurs next! What else did you bring?"

"There wasn't anything else special," said Tilly, looking in the basket again. "Only this big egg. It looks a bit old to me." It looked like an ordinary egg, but yellow with age, and with a musty, dusty smell about it. "It's not for tea, is it?"

Mrs Hardcastle lifted the egg gently out of the basket. "My lovely egg," she said.

"Is it very old?" asked Tilly.

"Very, very old. And very, very special. A magic egg from long ago. I keep it safe in memory . . ."

For a time the only thing that could be heard in the tree-room was the sound of the hedgehog babies snoring, and the barn owl rippling out his feathers.

"But it's no good crying over dead dodos," said Mrs Hardcastle. "That won't bring them back. Nothing will bring them back, Tilly. They're extinct."

"I wish they weren't," said Tilly. "I wish I could see one."

Mrs Hardcastle blew her nose and yawned. "Oh I'm feeling right dopey, Tilly Mint. I think it's time for my nap."

"Is it, Mrs Hardcastle?" said Tilly, a little bit excited, and a little bit scared. You never quite knew what was going to happen when Mrs Hardcastle went to sleep.

"Just for five minutes," Mrs Hardcastle said. She yawned again, a long achy, sighy sort of yawn that made the spiders huddle up for comfort in their silky webs. "By the way, Tilly. Watch out for the pirates, won't you?"

"Pirates!" said Tilly. But Mrs Hardcastle was already asleep, creaking backwards and forwards on her rocking chair, and snoring, very gently. One by one the rabbit and the hedgehogs and the badger and the mouse slipped away to their holes in the shelves and cupboards of Mrs Hardcastle's tree house.

Tilly lay down on the bed of downy feathers. She found a blanket made of leaves stitched together, and pulled it over herself.

Everything was silent now, except for the sound of Mrs Hardcastle's rocking chair creak-creak-creaking, and after a bit that became gentler, and slower, and softer, till it stopped altogether. Mice nibbled in their corners, and the barn-owl chicks fussed under their mother's wing. Deep below the tree roots a red fox stirred in his den, licked his dam and cubs, and slipped out into the night.

Tilly turned over, rustling her leaves. She couldn't sleep. She kept thinking about what Mrs Hardcastle had told her.

High above her the moon slid across the deep navy-blue of the sky. It glimmered down, down, through the branches of the trees, and through the hollow chimney of Mrs Hardcastle's tree house. It crept like pale seeping water down the twisted tree-trunk walls and across the pine-soft carpet, and when Tilly turned over again it had spilt in a silver gleam over Mrs Hardcastle's egg from long ago.

Chapter Three

The Egg from Long Ago

Tilly couldn't make out what it was at first.
The glow was as cold as a candle flame that's
just about to go out, or a moon reflected in
black water. She had to find out what it was.
She rustled out of her leaf-bed and tiptoed
over to the glow.

"It's the egg from long ago!" she
whispered.

She knelt down and touched it. "How cold
it is!" she said. "Poor egg from long ago! How
cold you are!" She picked it up in both
hands. It was as smooth as a pebble. She
tiptoed back to her leaf-bed and clambered
in, still hugging the egg, and then she
snuggled down so she and the egg were under
the leaf-blanket, warm and comfortable and
as soft as sleep.

And just as Tilly was drifting away on the
slow tide of Mrs Hardcastle's deep breathing
she heard a little tapping sound. It sounded as
if someone with a tiny chisel was knocking

on glass. *Tchink! Tchink!*

She listened, but she couldn't make it out at all. She snuggled the egg closer to her. It was warmer now, warmer than her hands. Even under the leaves she could see it was glowing gold. The tapping sounded again. *Tink-tink-tink.*

"It's not the egg, is it?" asked Tilly. And then she said, "No, of course it isn't."

The tapping came again.

"It is," Tilly said. "It's the egg. Shut up, egg. I can't sleep." And then she heard, as tiny as if it wasn't there at all, a "Cheep-cheep-cheep. Cheep." Tilly put her ear closer to the egg. It was almost as hot as a stone in the sunshine. There it came again. "Cheep," it went. "Cheep."

Tilly sat up. "It's the egg!" she shouted. "There's a noise in the egg! Mrs Hardcastle!" But Mrs Hardcastle was fast asleep, and would never hear her now.

"I think I'm a bit scared of eggs!" said Tilly.

The golden egg began to rock gently backwards and forwards, and then faster, and faster, and Tilly felt shivers of excitement like little rivers of lightning running up and down the back of her neck. She couldn't stop looking at the egg. A tiny crack had appeared in it, like a hair. As Tilly watched the shell began to splinter out from the crack.

Tilly dived back into the leaves and buried her face in them. "I'm not going to look!"

The cracking sound stopped. The rocking stopped. The glow had gone. Everything was still and silent again. Tilly lifted her head, and slowly opened her eyes.

"Hello," said a voice. "I don't suppose you're Tilly Mint, are you?"

Tilly sat up. A large bird, a bit like a turkey, was sitting next to her, shaking bits of shell off its feathers. Its beak was twisted round in what might be taken for a smile. It had yellow legs and big feet, and it was really quite fat.

"Yes, I am," said Tilly. "I don't suppose you're a turkey, are you?"

"Don't be silly, Tilly!" The bird jumped down and shook its feathers out, making the leaves swirl. "I believe turkeys are rather common birds." She put her head to one side. "Try again."

Tilly took a deep breath. She hardly dared say it, even though she knew with every bone in her body what this strange bird was.

"You couldn't be a dodo, could you?"

"Yes!" The bird clacked her beak with pride, and shook out her yellow wings as though she was plumping up a cushion. "You're quite right. I'm a dodo." She waddled about a bit, bending her legs now and again as if they were a bit stiff, and stretching out her feathers to straighten them up, like tired fingers. "And I can't tell you how glad I am to be out at last, after all those years!"

"But you can't really be a dodo," said Tilly. "Mrs Hardcastle told me that dodos are extinct."

The dodo stopped doing her exercises and

stared at Tilly. "Oh," she said, hurt. "Do I stink?"

"No, I don't mean that," said Tilly, though Dodo did smell a bit, she noticed. She had a funny, yolky, rotten-eggy smell about her, which wasn't surprising, really. "Extinct means you don't exist any more."

"Does it?" said Dodo. "Don't I?"

"But Dodo, you *do* exist," said Tilly. "You're here, and I can see you, so that must mean that you exist!" And she was so excited and pleased about it all that she jumped off the leaf-pile and flung her arms round her. The dodo bird squashed up like cotton wool and fluttered free, gasping for air.

"Don't do that!" she squawked. "You'll smother me!"

"I was trying to hug you," said Tilly. "Because I'm so happy to see you."

The dodo clucked deep in her throat, pleased, looking a bit pink for a bird. "People don't usually hug dodos, Tilly," she said shyly. "They hunt us, and they shoot us. Or they stuff us. They eat us, usually. But they never hug us. Never."

"They hunt you, Dodo? Why? Why would they do that?"

"I don't know," said Dodo sadly. "They

don't really seem to like us very much. We must be very ugly birds, I suppose."

She held out her stunted wings so Tilly could see her properly – her plump body, as grey as a pigeon; her shaggy feathers; her crooked, overgrown beak. Her stalky legs . . .

Tilly nodded.

"But we never did anybody any harm, you know."

"No," said Tilly. "I'm sure you didn't."

Dodo folded her wings down and put her head to one side, watching Tilly. "They've probably eaten us all by now, you know. That's what bothers me."

"But, Dodo, I don't understand. You're still here. I can see you." Tilly stroked the spiny feathers on Dodo's back, trying to comfort her.

"No, you don't understand, do you? I might be the only one left, you see. What's the good of being the only dodo in the world?" The dodo scrunched across the fragments of her shell, trying to sweep them up with her wing. It was as if she was trying to make an egg out of them again, so she could climb back in her shell and disappear.

She clucked unhappily. "I don't even know where I've hatched out. I want to go home!"

"Home!" said Tilly. "Where's that? I've no idea where your home is. It must be very far away."

"Over the hills and far away," agreed Dodo sadly. "Over the seas and through the skies. Into the wind and down the rain . . ."

"What do you mean, Dodo?" asked Tilly, puzzled.

"Back to the land of yesterday. Just to see if I can find any more dodos. Oh, Tilly, take me home."

"If only I could," said Tilly. "Back to the land of yesterday . . . because you're a bird of long ago. What a long, long way we'd have to go to get there, Dodo."

"It's all my fault," said the dodo. "Don't you worry about it, please. If I could fly, it might help. But I can't, you see . . ." She lifted her stubby wings out as far as they would go, and flapped them feebly. They didn't even lift her onto her toes. "Look at that!" she said. "I can't tell you how embarrassed I am about that, Tilly Mint. What's the good of being a bird if you can't even fly! What a mess!"

But Tilly was staring at her, trying to remember what Mrs Hardcastle had said to her . . . "*They're a bit like you, really. They don't know how to fly . . .*"

127

"But *I* can!" said Tilly. "Dodo, I can! I know how to fly! Mrs Hardcastle taught me! That's what the balloon and the feather were for, in her basket of special things. But she's asleep . . . If only I knew where she'd put them." She ran round in despair, looking under leaves and stones, and Dodo ran round after her, though she'd no idea what they were looking for, and at last, tired and fed up, Tilly put her hands deep into her pockets, and there they were.

"Here you are, Dodo," she said. "A balloon. And a feather."

Dodo cocked her head to one side to look at them, and then she cocked her head to the other side to get a better look, and pecked at them gently, and then she said, in a disappointed voice, "Yes, Tilly. Very nice."

"Mrs Hardcastle gave me this special feather, long ago, and I flew to the other side of the world with it," said Tilly. "And one day she gave me this balloon, and she said that only people who believed in magic could fly away with this."

"I've never even heard of magic," Dodo said.

Tilly slowly blew up the balloon.

"It's a sort of egg," said Dodo wistfully. She

tried to peck it, but Tilly jerked it away from her just in time.

"You mustn't pop it, whatever happens, or we'll never get going. Are you ready, Dodo?"

Dodo nodded.

"Right," said Tilly. "You'd better have the feather, because you're the bird.' She lifted up Dodo's wing and tucked the little blue feather under her armpit. "Don't drop it!" she warned. "Now. Hold onto my hand."

Dodo stretched her feathers out and placed them in Tilly's hand. Something of Tilly's excitement started to run through her, like zig-zaggings of lightning.

"I'm a bit scared, Tilly," she croaked.

"No, you're not," said Tilly. She held up her free hand, and the yellow balloon bobbed over her head on its piece of string.

"Where are we going?" asked Dodo.

"Up, I hope!" said Tilly. "Hold tight, Dodo! It's happening!"

The string grew taut, and Tilly and Dodo both rose up, wobbling, onto the tips of their toes.

"I think I'm going to be sick!" said Dodo faintly.

"No, you're not, Dodo!" shouted Tilly. "You're going to FLYYYYYYYYY!"

The bats opened their eyes and stared as they bobbed slowly towards them. The spiders ate up their webs in surprise. The barn owl in her nest turned her head right round and back again.

"A flying dodo!" squawked Dodo. "If only my mother could see me now!"

And a sudden wind rushed down the tall chimney of Mrs Hardcastle's tree house, swirling the swaying curtain leaves, whisking up the dusty pine needles, floating up the feathers on the downy bed, and with a huge *Whooooosh!* it lifted Tilly and Dodo up, up, to the very top of the tree.

And out they swung, all in a swirling rush, out above the tangle of high branches, up, up, and up, into the blue skies of the land of yesterday.

Chapter Four

Home Again, and Hunted

They landed almost straight away. It was a soft landing on sandy earth, and they were in brilliant sunshine. They stood up carefully, gazing round. They were surrounded by palm trees with tall scaly trunks and long-fingered palm leaves waving high above their heads.

"Hey! It's all different," Tilly said slowly. "This doesn't look right to me."

"It does to me," said Dodo happily. "It looks just right to me. It looks just the place to find dodos." She scurried round bushes that were vivid with deep red and purple flowers. "Have you seen the dodos?" she clucked to the little creatures that seemed to be nesting deep in the green heart of the bushes. "Have you seen anyone who looks like me?"

She stopped suddenly and lifted up first one wing and then the other, and peered into her armpits, and then clapped her wings across her beak. "Tilly! I've lost it!

I've dropped your feather!"

"Don't worry, Dodo." Tilly was much too excited about finding the far-away land of the dodos to be worried about that. "I've still got the balloon, remember. We'll be all right."

She tied the balloon to a knobble on the tree trunk, where it bobbed like a reflection of the huge yellow sun. A chattering in the branches above her head startled her. She looked up to see a bird as bright as flames peering down at her.

"Look and see!" it shrieked. "Come and see and look at this!"

More birds fluttered down to join it. The air buzzed with the hum of their wings and flashed with the lights of their jewel colours. Monkeys swung along the branches to join them, and dangled by their long arms, jabbering to each other and pointing. A striped snake coiled itself like a spring unwinding round a log, and lay, quiet as secrets, with its quick tongue flickering.

"Well!" said Dodo. "Look at this! Look at this, Tilly Mint! All my friends have come to meet me."

The fire-bird floated down and circled above Dodo's head. Then it flew right up to her and pecked her on her fat cheek.

"Oi!" squawked Dodo. "That hurt!"

The red bird flew up and up again until it had lifted itself right over the palm trees.

"They're dodos!" it screeched. "The dodos are back! The dodos are back!"

The cry was taken up by all the other birds, and by the monkeys, and by the hissing snake, and by the buzzing insects and all the other little creatures in the bushes. "The dodos are back!"

Dodo smiled her beaky smile. She darted from one bush to another, reaching up and crouching down to peck and nuzzle the creatures there.

"The dodos are back!" she sang. "Hurray! The dodos are back!"

Tilly felt herself being nudged forward until she stood right in the middle of the dancing ring, and then one of her hands was taken by a monkey and the other by a black boar and without being able to stop herself she was lifting up her feet and dancing to the whistles of the birds.

"I'm not a dodo, you know," she kept saying. "I'm really Tilly Mint." But it didn't seem to matter. They all seemed just as pleased to see her as they were to see the dodo. Dodo stood in the middle of it all and tilted back her head and crowed with joy to be home again.

But it was the fire-bird who put an end to the dancing. He'd been circling high over their heads, and his shrill alarm call froze them as if winter clouds had blotted out their sun.

"Hide away! Hide away! The hunters, the hunters, the hunters are here!"

Up the birds flew, and away the animals scampered, and all the brilliant bushes trembled into quietness again.

"Oh dear!" said Dodo. "Where've they all gone?"

"I think they're hiding," said Tilly.

"What a shame. I was enjoying myself then, Tilly. Weren't they nice!"

"They were very nice," Tilly agreed. "But I didn't see any dodos with them."

"No, neither did I," Dodo sighed. "But I'm sure they'll be around somewhere. Perhaps they've gone somewhere. To sleep, I should think. That'll be where they've gone. Dodos love dozing. I'll go and find them, shall I? You stay here and hide and I'll go and find all my dodo friends and bring them to see you. I know you'll like them."

"Be careful!" Tilly begged her.

Dodo scurried away from her, too excited to listen, and calling out to anything that might happen to be within hearing distance. "Have you seen any dodos? Have you seen anyone round here who looks like me? Quite a nice bird, tall, you know, and rather charming actually . . ."

"Caw! Caw! Caution!" A huge grey bird with yellow eyes and a hooded head swooped down and lifted Dodo up between its talons.

"Help me! I've fallen off the world!" screamed Dodo.

The grey bird clapped its wing across her beak. "Don't you dodos ever learn!" it hissed. "There's danger down there. Danger!" It perched her among the fronds at the top of the palm tree.

Tilly tried to climb after them, but her arms were aching after all that flying, and she couldn't seem to lift them up high enough. She scrabbled frantically at the sides of the tree. She was alone, and the sounds of danger were growing closer.

"Hide!" the grey bird screeched.

Tilly looked round wildly. She could hear the stealthy movements of the hunter. She could just see him now as he crouched through the bushes holding a net out on a long stick in front of him. Insects throbbed round her ears.

"Dizguize yourzel," they buzzed.

She backed into a low, sprawling bush that was heavy with hanging flowers, and bright with butterflies.

"Be zafe! Dizguize!" the insects sizzled.

If I was a butterfly I'd be safe! she thought.

136

I know I would. No one would harm a
butterfly.

The zizzing of the insects grew louder in
her head. A hazy cloud of pale blue butterflies
flittered round her. She felt the strange
sensation of growing down and down till she
was tiny, and light as air. Her arms stretched
up over her head, and felt as if they were
spreading out like fans, and lifting her up
with slow beats. She was drifting up from the
ground. Air rippled round her like water . . .

A rich, heavy perfume rose up and she
realized that she had landed on the silky
petals of a flower, and that her beating
arms had come to rest. She could just turn
her head enough to see that she had wings of
vivid gold with flashes and swirls of crimson,
and that they were as delicate as painted silk.
And she saw something else. She saw the
huge pale pink face of the hunter peering
down at her.

"I've never seen a butterfly like this
before!" he said. "I must have it for my
collection."

"I'm not a butterfly!" Tilly tried to shout.
"I'm only Tilly Mint!" But her voice made
no sound at all.

She flickered her wings anxiously, trying

to lift herself away from the flower and the looming face. But she was too late, and too tiny. The man swung his net over her as she fluttered up. She was trapped.

Chapter Five

The Spell of the Lizard

"Save her! Save her!" the grey bird screamed.
"Save Dodo's friend!"

The buzzing of the insects rose to a high,
angry howl, and they swarmed like a black
cloud round the man and his net. He flapped
his arms to try to fan them away from his
face. Tilly felt herself being buffeted about in
the net, and somersaulting upside down, so
that her breath bumped out of her and her
wings felt bruised and shredded. Every time
she managed to crawl to the top of the net
she tumbled down again.

"Save her!" the bird cried.

Then the insects with stings in their tails
closed round the hunter. They landed on his
skin and jabbed at him angrily, so that his
flesh came up in big red bumps. They fizzed
round his eyes and his ears, and dive-bombed
at his nose. They swarmed along the sweat-
sticky edges of his shirt collar and his cuffs.
And at last he dropped his net and ran for

cover, his arms across his face and the black
cloud buzzing round his head.

Pieces of wing like flower petals drifted
down to the ground. Tilly, bruised and
breathless, crawled out of the net. She would
never fly now, with broken wings. Someone
could tread on her, easily.

"You had a lucky escape there." A papery
voice crackled, close to her ear.

"Hide!" the grey bird screeched again.
"More hunters! Hide!"

Tilly tried to hop up the trunk of the palm
tree.

"That isn't the way to hide!" the papery
voice crackled again. "You can be seen a mile
off, with all those colours."

"I wish I could turn into Tilly again," Tilly
sighed. "But I don't know how to."

"Don't do that," said the voice. "Tillys are
much too big to hide."

"Then how can I hide?" Tilly could hear
the snapping of twigs that meant that more
hunters were coming.

The paper voice tickled her ear. "Like me!"
it said. "Look like me, Tilly! That's best."

Tilly looked round the tree in the direction
of the voice, but all she could see was
knobbly trunk, and scaly brown bark, and

nothing at all that could speak.

"I'm sorry, but I can't see you!" she whispered back. "I can't tell where you are!"

"That's the idea," the voice scratched. "Look again, on your left."

Tilly looked. The tree seemed to slit its bark a tiny way, and something like a brown eye glinted out, and then closed up again. The crackle laughed. "Saw me then, didn't you?"

"Yes," said Tilly. "I can see where you are, but I can't see *what* you are! You're not a talking tree, are you? A talking, winking sort of tree?"

The cackle laughed again. "Look again, and you'd better be quick, or you'll miss me."

Tilly looked again, just to her left, and this time she saw the tiny crack again, and the gleam of an eye, then another crack, and the gleam of another eye; a quick flick that showed a tail, and a tiny dart forward, and then stillness again, and nothing to see but tree trunk.

"I think I saw something," she said. "I think I saw something like a lizard, just for a second."

"So you did," the papery voice crinkled, disappointed. "You must have better eyesight than I thought. Or maybe I'm getting old, Tilly. I used to be very good at disguises."

It opened its eyes again, and very clearly was a lizard, scaly-skinned and flick-tailed, and then it closed them and turned back to tree bark.

"You do it, Tilly," he said. "It's the best way to hide."

"But how did you do it?" asked Tilly.

"Ah, that's my secret. Lizards are like wizards. Didn't you know that?"

"No," said Tilly, feeling weak and trembly. Her skin was growing tight and stretched. Her broken butterfly wings had floated down to the ground, and her arms were tucking up under her body. "What's happening to me, Lizard?"

"Something wizardy," the dry voice scratched. "Don't even think about it. Just close your eyes, Tilly Lizard, and listen to the chant:

"Lizards are like wizards,
We're as old
As magic spell.

We're flickery and tricksy
and whispery and wise

142

We're firelight and waterfall
And lightning in disguise

We're the keepers
Of the secrets
In holes of shell and bone

Where moles creep
Where owls sleep
In crack of tree and stone

Lizards are like wizards,
We're as old
As magic spell.

Never told
Never tell."

"Quiet down there!" hissed the grey bird. "Hunters!"

Tilly breathed in and squeezed herself flat against the tree, and now she could hear a quiet rustling in the bushes, a creak and snap of twigs as two hunters came pushing through a tangle of bushes and stopped for a rest in the shade of the very tree that she was clinging to. They leaned against it. She breathed softly, knowing that she was in disguise now; hidden, and safe.

Over their heads Dodo sat, dizzily swaying

on the branch, with the grey bird's wing stuffed into her beak. "I'd goid do fall off id a midid," she tried to say, and was ignored.

The first of the hunters was a skinny man who looked as if he hadn't had a decent meal for months. He carried a wriggling sack slung over his shoulder, and when he stopped he let it fall roughly to the ground. A brown paw poked out of a hole in the sack, and he kicked it.

"Now then," said the other hunter, a tall man with a nose like a hook. He carried a gun across his shoulder. "They won't be fit for eating if you tread on them."

"I can soon catch more, if I wants to."

"Let's have a look at them," said the tall man. He peered into the sack. "What's the use of catching little things like that? I go in for the wild stuff. Big Game." He sighed. "Not that I've caught anything here."

"That's because you're noisy. Never catch nothing if you're noisy. Got to go quiet, got to go creepy, got to scuttle like a leaf in the wind."

"Ah, just you wait and see, I'll be the first to catch the dodo. Just you wait and see."

The two men sat back with their arms folded, happily dreaming about the dodo

they were going to catch. They didn't hear
the little worried screech up in the branch
above them, though Tilly did. She flicked an
eye open quickly, and flicked it shut again.

"Will you know a dodo when you sees
one, that's the thing," said the skinny man.
"They're very rare."

"Of course I'll know a dodo!" the tall one
said. "It's a great big, monster sort of thing,
very fierce of course, with snappy teeth. And

it growls. When I catch it I'm going to stuff it and hang it on my wall. Did you hear something squeak just then?"

The other man listened and shook his head. "Not a thing. Now, if I catches the dodo, I'm going to eat it. I've heard they're ugly flappy birds, but nice and fat!"

"Listen! Another squeak! Did you hear that?" They both strained to listen.

The skinny man went on, "And, what's more, they're very easy to catch, so I'm told. Do you know, they're so stupid, they can't even fly! Whoever heard of a bird that can't fly!"

They both seemed to find this very amusing, in fact they were laughing so much that they didn't even hear the third hunter arrive. Tilly could just see him if she slit her eye open. It was the butterfly collector. He was rubbing his arms and his neck where the insects had stung him.

"I can hear you, laughing about dodos," he scowled. "You needn't think you can catch one of them, you know."

"Why not?"

"Because they're extinct!"

This time the squeak came loud and clear and indignant.

"DODO EGGS DON'T STINK!"

Many things happened then. The hunters all set off in different directions in search of the screech. The skinny one tripped over his bag, and a dozen little hairy creatures like guinea-pigs with long legs and silky rabbity ears scuttled out.

"My mole-rats!" he shouted. "I've lost my dinner."

The butterfly collector swung his net round to try and catch them as they darted in and out of all the legs. And the tall hook-nose, the great hunter of Big Game, stuck his gun up into the air and closed his eyes and fired.

Dodo fell from her tree like a stone dropping from a cliff, and landed with a thud in the bushes.

For a moment, everything was as still as sleep.

"Did you see that!" the tall hunter shouted, his voice strangled with amazement. "I shot it! I killed it!"

"Oh no! Oh no! Dodo!" Tilly cried. She scuttled down from the tree, and realized she was scurrying on little lizardy legs. "You've shot Dodo!" she shouted, and her voice scrunched like crackly paper, tiny and useless and mad with grief. "Why did you shoot

Dodo? She never did anyone any harm!"

She flicked her scaly tail like a whip and
skittered under the feet of the three hunters as
they ran to pick Dodo up. But when they
looked inside the bush, the dodo had gone.
They searched round it, and under it, and
because Tilly was so small she could slide
right among its roots. It was true. The dodo
had gone.

"Botheration!" said the tall one. "That was
my best prize. I could have stuffed it and kept
it on my mantelpiece."

"I could have eaten it up. It was so fat it
would have lasted me for a week," said the
thin one.

"I could have put it in a cage and sold it
to a zoo," said the collector. "I'd have been
famous then."

"Botheration!" the Big Game hunter said
again, and he held his gun up in the air and
closed his eyes and fired, at anything at all,
just to make a noise, he was so angry; and
there came an answering bang that was
even louder than his, and something floated
down on a piece of string, something
yellow and tattered and rubbery. The
hunter looked at it in amazement.

"By Jove!" he said. "I've shot two

birds in one day."

"Funny-looking bird to me," said the collector. He picked it up and turned it over and over in his hand. "Wish you hadn't killed it. It would have looked good in my collection." He peered up at the tree. "Wonder if it's got a nest up there?"

"Let's have a look at it," the thin one said. He pulled its skin to make it stretch, and sniffed it. Then he sucked it and spat it out again. "I'm not eating that."

"Can't even stuff it," the tall one said. "Never mind. It was probably very dangerous. It's probably just as well I did shoot it." He marched off, whistling, pleased with himself, with his gun slung over his shoulder, and the other two followed him with their empty sack and net slung over theirs.

When their footsteps had died away, Tilly crawled back out of the bush, slow and heavy with sadness. She squeezed her eyes shut against the sunlight and let her hot tears roll down her cheeks and onto the dusty earth.

Chapter Six

Down Among the Mole-rats

"I've never seen a lizard cry before."

Tilly opened one of her eyes. A small brown monkey was crouched on all fours beside her, with its head touching the ground and turned to one side so that it could peer right into her face.

"Don't cry, Lizard," the monkey said.

Tilly sniffed. "I'm not a lizard really. I'm Tilly Mint." Another tear wobbled down her lumpy face. "That's one of the things I'm crying about."

"Never mind." The monkey put out a paw and gently dabbed up the tear. "I like lizards."

Tilly hiccupped. "Thank you."

The monkey lay down on one side so it could talk to Tilly more comfortably. "What else are you crying about, Tilly Mint?"

Tilly took a deep breath. "They've killed Dodo," she whispered. "And she's disappeared. And they've shot my balloon, so I can't fly home again. And I've turned into a lizard."

It was all so much and so terrible that she

couldn't stop her tears coming again, and all the kind monkey could do to help was to pat her head and dab her tears away.

"I'm sure everything will be all right," she said.

A shadow hovered over them, cold as clouds, and although Tilly couldn't lift up her head to look at it she recognized its screech.

"I saw it all. I saw the dodo fall," the grey bird called.

"Where is she now, then?" asked the monkey. "This Tilly Lizard is very upset about her."

"They carried her away," the grey bird screamed. "Down the dark caves. Away, away." And the shadow shifted away from them and flitted back up into the trees.

"Who did?" asked Tilly.

"The mole-rats!" the grey bird screeched, high up in the treetops. "Lifted her up on their backs and ran away with her. Down the dark caves."

"The mole-rats!" said Tilly. "They were the animals that escaped from the hunter's bag! Monkey, can you show me where the mole-rats live?"

"Of course I can, Tilly!" The monkey did a handstand, delighted that one of Tilly's problems at least had been solved. "I should

have thought of that! They wouldn't have
wanted the hunters to chop poor old Dodo
up, you see. Or stuff her. Sorry, Tilly. But
those people do terrible things to animals,
they really do."

"But where do the mole-rats live?"

"Here!" the monkey chuckled, dancing
again. "Here and here and here!"

And she pointed to holes under the tree
roots.

Tilly scuttled to the edge of one of the
holes. "Down there? But it's dark, and deep,
and cold down there. Monkey, will you come
down with me?" she asked.

But the monkey swung up the nearest tree,
somersaulting from branch to branch. "Not
me, Tilly Lizard!" she laughed. "I like to play
in the sunshine. Don't like dark holes, cold
and creepy. Bye, Tilly Lizard! Good luck! I'm
sure everything will be all right!"

And though Tilly couldn't see her any
more, she could see the monkey's shadow
swinging by its long arms from tree to tree.

She peered down the hole again. She
could even smell the musky cool dampness.

I wonder if lizards like dampness, she
thought, and taking a deep breath, she slid
down into the black mouth of the hole.

It wasn't too bad at first. There was plenty of
light filtering through to show her the way,
and she could see the marks of little paws,
and a scoop in the earth where something
had been dragged along. But when she came
to a bend in the tunnel the light stopped
altogether, and she was darting along in
darkness. When she came to a fork in the
tunnel she nearly turned back again.

"Now which way? Which way? Which
way? Way? Way?" her lizardy voice echoed.

153

"Who's that? Who's that? That? That? That?" a scared voice piped.

"Me," whispered Tilly, trying to stop the echoes bouncing. "It's only me."

Something furry thrust up against her nose, nearly treading on her.

"Don't do that," said Tilly. "You'll squash me."

The paw moved, and she felt a wet nose snuffling her.

"Ah, it's a lizard," the voice said. "You'll have to turn back, I'm afraid. They don't like lizards down there. Not much."

"But I'm not a lizard," said Tilly. "I'm Tilly Mint really."

"I still can't let you in. It's more than my job's worth. Only mole-rats allowed past this point."

'And dodos?" asked Tilly hopefully.

"I believe I did see a dodo once, yes," the mole-rat guard said. "Bit fat for down here."

"Was it just now that you saw her?"

"Might have been," said the guard cautiously. "Why d'you want to know?"

"Because she's my friend," said Tilly. "Was, I mean. Was my friend." She couldn't stop her voice from wobbling.

"Now, now. Don't do that," the mole-rat

begged. "You'll set me off, and once you've set me off you never stop me. I'm that soft-hearted . . ." He wiped his nose on the furriest bit of his arm.

"Then please let me go on," said Tilly.

"Couldn't you do something about this lizard business?" asked the mole-rat. "They'd be very upset if I let a lizard go down there."

It was hopeless. What Tilly would have liked more than anything would have been to turn back into Tilly Mint again, but that would have been no use at all. She'd have been well and truly stuck if that happened. She'd have to stay there for ever, or till she got very thin . . .

"It's more than my job's worth, you see," he explained. "I daren't let you past, and that's that." Tilly could hear him stroking his beardy chin. "Perhaps there's something else I could do for you? You've come all this way – it seems a shame to send you back again so soon. I could sing you a song, if you like. Would that cheer you up a bit?"

"Not very much," Tilly sniffed. And then she had an idea. "I mean yes," she said. "It would cheer me up a lot."

"I love singing," said the mole-rat. "Better than eating, or digging, or going for long

155

walks by a river. I love singing songs. What number would you like?"

"Erm . . ." said Tilly.

"Have song number seventy-five," the mole-rat suggested. "It's my favourite."

"All right," said Tilly.

The mole-rat began to sing immediately, in the sweet, high, whistling tone of a choirboy, and now Tilly could see a little better she could just make him out, poised on his back legs with his front paws pressed together across his fuzzy chest, and his head held high, and his eyes closed.

"All things begin in darkness
In shell, in nut, in hole,
In seed, in spawn, in nest, in soil,
We thank the makers of us all.

And so our grateful song we raise
Sing out of darkness in their praise
With squeaks and chirps and croaks and roars
With wings and fins and paws and claws.

We thank the earth, our mother,
We thank the sun, our father,
For giving us each other
And the precious gift of life."

The mole-rat's voice echoed round and round the dark tunnels, sweet and clear as water tumbling over stones. And while he was singing, with his paws still pressed together and his eyes closed, Tilly crept past him, quiet as ripples, and down the main tunnel, and as she began to pick up speed she heard him change his tune to a piping, jigging, skipping song that set him dancing and helped her to run as fast as her long-toed feet would take her.

She didn't stop running until she saw a glow at the end of the tunnel. At first she thought she'd run right through it, and that she'd met daylight again, but then she realized that the tunnel swung round a bend and that the glow came from thousands of little insects, all fluttering and shimmering along the tunnel walls and lighting up a large underground cavern. As she crept nearer, the glow became so brilliant that she was dazzled by it.

From far away at the guard's end of the tunnel she could hear his voice still trilling a jig, and the stamp of his feet as he danced to it in the darkness. Now as she broke through into the green and gold brilliance of the cavern, the same tune was echoing round and round. Dozens of mole-rats were dancing round to it, whirling each other shoulder high, singing away in high piping voices, leaping round in mad circles, and high above their voices another voice was squawking, loud and froggy and cheerful.

Tilly pressed herself down to peer under the skipping feet. Lying on her back in the middle of the ring, waving her legs about in time to the music, and with her feathers nearly black with dust, was Dodo.

Chapter Seven

Danger Everywhere

Tilly darted into the middle of the circle of dancing mole-rats. "Dodo!" she cried.

The mole-rats froze in stillness.

Dodo did her best to sit up, though the roof of the cavern was too low for this. She tried to twist her head round and got her beak stuck. "Did fomeone fpeak?"

"I did!" said Tilly. "It's me, Tilly Mint! Oh, Dodo, I'm so glad you're still alive."

"Of courfe I'm ftill alive!" said Dodo to the roof.

"I thought the hunters had shot you! They didn't hurt you, did they?"

"Didn't touch me!" said Dodo proudly, freeing her beak at last. "To tell you the truth, Tilly, all that happened was that I went a little dizzy from being so high up, you know, and a bit excited I expect, and well, I fainted. I fell off the tree and next thing I knew I woke up lying on my back and being rushed along headfirst through the bushes, and then pushed down a hole, and then dragged along tunnels till I thought my head was going to come right off, and here I am at last .. and, Tilly, these dear friends did it all, and they've rescued me from the hunters."

Tilly looked round and saw that the mole-rats were standing in a line staring at her, nibbling rapidly as though they'd got things stuck between their teeth, and whispering to each other. She was worried. The guard had told her that they didn't like lizards much. What would they do to her?

They lowered their blunt flat heads like battering rams and moved slowly towards her.

Her heart started to thump in her throat. "Hello," she said, and she noticed how her voice had stopped being crackly and was suddenly squeaky with nerves. "I'm Tilly Mint really."

The largest mole-rat, who was pure white with big red eyes and fine quivering whiskers, stepped out of the line and came up to Tilly Mint, sniffing right up to her face. At last she stepped back, as if she was satisfied. "Hello, Tilly Mint," she said. Her voice was soft and silky, like a cat purring. "I'm the queen of the mole-rats, and I'm very happy that you've

160

come to visit us."

She nodded to the others. Tilly found
herself surrounded by mole-rats all sniffing
round her so that they tickled her with their
whiskers, and one or two of them began to
lick her with quick, busy jabs of their tongue,
making her want to giggle.

"Listen to me," said the white queen of the
mole-rats seriously. "I am very pleased to
meet you, Tilly Mint, because you seem to be
a friend of the dodo bird's, and she's very
special to us. But how did you get in? Usually
only mole-rats and wounded animals in great
danger can come down here. You smell of
humans, and they're our greatest enemy. You
also smell of lizards, and we don't like them
much either. I can tell there's no danger
about you . . . but how did you get past the
guard?"

"He didn't want me to get past him!" said
Tilly. "He told me not to. But I had to find
Dodo."

The queen sniffed at Tilly again, then
padded round her, deep in thought.

"Then how did you get past him?"

"It wasn't his fault," said Tilly. "Really it
wasn't. You mustn't blame him. He didn't see
me go past him."

The queen swung round and padded round Tilly in the opposite direction. It made Tilly dizzy to watch her. "He didn't see you!" She stopped and faced Tilly. "This is very serious. Tell me. If he didn't see you . . . was it because he had his eyes closed?"

"Yes," whispered Tilly.

"Was he singing, Tilly Mint?"

"Yes."

The queen stopped. "I thought so! I thought so!" she shouted. "He must be punished!"

"No!" cried Tilly. "Please don't punish him! It was my fault. I asked him to sing."

The queen wasn't listening to her. She ran to two young mole-rats. "You!" she said. "Go to the entrance and fetch the guard to me. And you! Take his place at the entrance to our burrow. And remember . . . Never close your eyes! Never sing on duty! Let no stranger pass!" The two mole-rats scampered off out of the lit cavern into the darkness of the burrow.

The queen sighed. "It is a very serious matter," she told Tilly. "Every second of our lives we must watch out for danger. The only peace we can hope to have is when we're here, resting in our cavern. What hope for us

is there if our guard lets strangers through?
Do you understand, Tilly Mint? This is the
great hall of the mole-rats. Here are young
mole-rats who are learning to hunt and dig
and help us all to survive. And here are old
mole-rats, who've spent their lives in service
to the pack, and who deserve to rest
peacefully, out of harm's way. And here are
mother mole-rats nursing their young. See the
babies, Tilly Mint?"

In the quiet corners of the great hall Tilly
could see mothers bent over little pink
bundles, and she could hear the tiny squeaks
of the babies as they opened up their mouths
for food.

"Now do you understand, Tilly Mint? I
must make sure that they're protected. I must!
I must!"

Tilly nodded. Behind her, Dodo sniffed into
her feathers. "Nobody's safe!" she said.

"No," agreed the mole-rat queen. "Not
when man's around. There's danger
everywhere."

They could hear a scampering down the
tunnel that led to the great hall, and then
behind it a slow dragging sound, like
someone limping, and soon into the light the
young mole-rat ran, and behind him limped

the guard, his head bent, his whiskers trailing in the dust, all the song and the jigging gone from him.

"Come here, Guard," said the white queen sternly.

Slowly the guard walked over to her. "I'm sorry, Queen," he said hoarsely. He bowed his head.

"Sorry!" the queen shouted. "Sorry!" Her voice echoed in the great hall, and fled tumbling down all the dark tunnels that led off from it.

Tilly turned away and buried her head in Dodo's side. She couldn't bear to look. "Don't hurt him!" she begged. "Don't hurt him."

Then she realized that the queen was talking to the guard again, but softly, soft as a cat, kind and sad and gentle.

"You have failed us, Old Guard," she said to him. "We could have been killed. Remember the time the hunters came with dogs? Do you remember that time, Old Guard?"

"Yes, Queen."

Tilly could hardly hear him.

"Tell us what happened, Old Guard, in case any of us has forgotten. I was only a mole-ratling then. But you remember, Guard.

What happened?"

The older mole-rats huddled together and moaned, remembering terrible things. But the younger ones scampered up to the guard and gathered round him, wanting a story. The mothers hushed their whimpering babies so they could listen.

"It was four or five summers ago," said the old guard. His voice was heavy and sad, as if he was telling a story that should never be forgotten. "Some hunters came to the island with dogs and guns. They shot many of our fine animals. They put many in cages to take away in boats to distant lands. All the creatures hid where they could, terrified for their lives, too frightened to go out for food.

"We mole-rats came in our hundreds to this great hall and cowered down in the darkness here. We didn't dare let the insects light it up for us even. We lay in the darkness for days and days, listening, listening out for danger. We had a guard at every entrance, and all the strong mole-rats were ready to rush out and defend the pack as soon as they got word of danger. Not a sound down here, for nights on end.

"And then, one night, a dog broke through and came sneaking down one of the tunnel entrances without any of us hearing him. As soon as he got to the great hall he leapt on us with a howling and a lashing of his legs and a terrible clashing together of his great yellow teeth. He killed the queen . . ."

"I know," the queen nodded. "My grandmother. He killed my grandmother . . ."

"And he sent all the mole-rats fleeing for their lives down the tunnels, fleeing in every direction, and outside all the entrances men were waiting with guns to shoot us as we came out . . ."

"And many of our brothers and sisters were killed that day," put in one of the very old mole-rats. "I was a baby, clinging onto my mother's back. She was killed."

"Many, many were killed." The queen nodded. Her voice was very quiet in the tunnel. "You've remembered it well, Old Guard. And can you remember one last thing? Can you remember how the hunter's dog got past the guard?"

It was a long time before the guard spoke again. He cleared his throat. "Yes, Queen, I can remember," he said. "The guard was asleep."

"Exactly," said the queen. "The guard was asleep. He had his eyes closed."

In the silence that followed, Tilly crept away from Dodo and went over to the old guard. She put her arms round his neck. "I can see that Guard must be punished," she said. "But if you punish him, you must punish me as well, because I had to get past him to find Dodo. I'd have found a way somehow."

"Oh dear," said Dodo. "Then I suppose it's all my fault for fainting. And it's the grey bird's fault for putting me in the tree. And it's the hunter's fault for coming here in the first place."

"Yes!" chorused the old mole-rats, who'd grown up with the guard and who'd always been his friends, and jigged to his tunes as well, on their way down the tunnels. "It's the hunter's fault. Blame the hunter!"

"Quiet!" shouted the queen. All the squeaks and shouts stopped. "I must think about his punishment. Quiet!"

For a long time the queen paced the floor of the cavern while the waiting mole-rats shuffled and coughed and the babies murmured in their sleep. At last the queen stopped. Everyone's eyes were on her.

"His punishment," she announced, "is that he will never, never, be allowed to guard the mole-rats again."

Everyone nodded, even the old guard, at the justice of this punishment. He shuffled round to the back of the old mole-rats and stood there, head hung low, ashamed.

"And what about his reward?" demanded Dodo.

"Reward?" said the queen. "How can I reward him for what he did?"

"He helped Tilly to find me again."

"And he's got a lovely singing voice," said Tilly. "He ought to be rewarded for having such a nice voice. And he sang me a very important song."

"Sing it!" demanded the queen.

So the old mole-rat guard shuffled forward again, and a bit timidly at first, and then growing more confident, he sang the song he'd sung at the entrance to the tunnel. His voice was pure and sweet, even for such an old mole-rat, and all the other mole-rats sang softly behind him, and the queen swayed backwards and forwards, and so did Dodo, still on her back.

"Beautiful!" they all said, when the old guard had shuffled back behind the line again.

"Your reward," said the queen, purring again, "is to take on the important and

dangerous task of escorting Tilly Mint and
Dodo out through the tunnels and back to
daylight, where they belong."

The old guard hobbled forward joyfully.
"With pleasure, Queen. Queen of the Night.
White Lady of the Shadows. Moon of the
Darknesses . . ."

"Now, now," she purred. "Don't get carried
away. Take great care of them, old friend.
Tilly Mint is a special visitor from England.
Look after her. And Dodo . . ." She looked at
Dodo, who was struggling to turn round onto
her stomach, with the help of Tilly and some
of the stronger mole-rats. ". . . Dodo is the
most precious creature on the island. She may
be the last of her kind. Take care! Take great
care!"

Dodo was at last sorted out, and with a lot
of fussing and squawking on her part and
shouts and shoves from everyone else, she was
pushed out of the great hall and into a tunnel
that broadened out and up so that she could
at least crawl.

"Goodbye, Queen Mole-rat," said Tilly.
"Thank you very much for your help."

"Goodbye, Tilly Mint." The queen sniffed
her so closely that her damp nose touched
Tilly's cheek, and her quivering whiskers

brushed her face. "There is great danger ahead of you," she whispered. "But there's nothing more we can do to help you. Beware of the pirates, Tilly Mint! Beware! Beware!"

She stood back and Tilly ran to catch up with Dodo and Mole-rat. "Goodbye, Tilly Mint!" all the little mole-rats called, jigging along the tunnel behind them as far as they dared. "Goodbye, Dodo."

"Goodbye!" Dodo called gaily. "Tilly, I can't tell you how good it is to be on my feet again! And we're off to the sunshine! Hooray!"

Old Mole-rat started to sing one of his jigging songs, and Dodo skipped happily beside him, knocking her head now and then on low bits of the tunnel, and tripping over Mole-rat's tail, and behind them ran Tilly, with the queen mole-rat's warning ringing in her head.

"Beware of the pirates, Tilly Mint! Beware! Beware!"

Chapter Eight

Beware of the Pirates

It was a long time before they began to see daylight. For hours they seemed to twist and twine through dark, damp tunnels, and though Mole-rat never stopped singing his voice began to grow weak and hoarse, and he stopped jigging and took up his dragging limp again. Dodo gave up trying to skip, and Tilly trailed a long way behind.

"I don't like it here much," she said. "I don't like the darkness."

That started poor old tired Mole-rat singing his favourite song again:

"All things begin in darkness
In shell, in nut, in hole,
In seed, in spawn, in nest, in soil . . ."

and it was then that Tilly began to make out the beginning of daylight. It came like a tiny pinprick far away, and then it was like an eye, then a moon, and then the light came bursting through, flooding the tunnel as if it was water rushing through it. The roof of the tunnel grew higher and higher, yet Tilly found she was having to stoop as she ran, and she realized that she could see her own Tilly Mint feet again in their stripy socks and shoes. She was well over the heads of Dodo and Mole-rat.

At last they were out of the tunnel. They seemed to be standing in a cave, and outside it they could hear the shush of the sea.

Dodo staggered against Tilly, exhausted. "Phew!" she laughed. "That was fun! Aren't we having fun these days, Tilly Mint!"

Mole-rat looked up at Tilly. "You've grown a bit," he said anxiously. "You look a bit like a human now."

"I am a human," said Tilly. "I'm a little girl."

"She doesn't act like one though," Dodo promised him. 'She acts more like a mole-rat."

Tilly ran out of the cave onto the yellow sands of a beach. "Look at this!" she shouted. "I'm going to paddle!" She kicked off her shoes and socks and waded into the blue-green water, and it lapped round her ankles as if it was trying to lick life back into her tired feet.

"Just the job!" shouted Mole-rat, and plunged in after her, paddling madly with all four feet at once. "Haven't swum since I was a ratling!" He bobbed down and flicked over, waving his stubby legs in the air, and bobbed back over again.

"Come on in, Dodo-my-duckling!" he shouted. "Get those feathers wet!"

Dodo shook her head shyly. "Can't swim," she said.

"I'll splash you if you don't!" Mole-rat scampered out onto the sands and shook himself, spraying her like a fountain. She screeched and flapped her short wings at him.

"Stop it, now, stop it, Mole-rat," she scolded. "Act your age! Behave yourself!"

"I only want you to enjoy yourself, Dodo-of-my-dreams!" he said. "Come and wash your corns! And watch out for jellyfish!"

He scurried back into the sea, splashing Tilly as he ran past her, and struck out across the little bay, gurgling as he went:

"Proper little squelchy things
Blobs of slime
Pink and purple bubbles
Dancers in the brine
Swirling out their skirtses

Watch them do their curtsies
Swaying in the waves like washing on the
   line . . ."

Tilly started after him. "I know that song!"
she shouted.

"Sing it then, Tilly-Winkle!" he called back
to her, but she gazed after his little splashing
head, trying to remember where she'd heard
the song before, and who had sung it to her.

Meanwhile Dodo had stepped carefully
onto a large knobbly stone that was just at
the water's edge, and sat there preening
herself. She splayed out her stumpy wings,
shaking the dust off her feathers, and pecked
them smooth again.

"Everything's all right now, isn't it, Tilly?"
she said.

"Yes," said Tilly. "It seems to be." She lay
on her back in the warm, kind water, and
looked up at the blue sky with gulls wheeling
over her head. It did seem then that
everything was all right again. The water
rocked her gently.

Suddenly Dodo shrieked: "Help me! Help
me! I've been kidnapped!"

Tilly sat up in the water. Dodo had gone!
She ran out onto the shore.

"Not that way!" Dodo squawked. "Out here! Out here!"

Tilly turned round and saw Dodo flapping on her stone, which was briskly walking out to sea.

"I didn't know stones could swim!" wailed Dodo, as the stone lifted up its leathery flippers and floated off.

"I'm not a stone, I'm a turtle," said the turtle. "Can't sit about sunbathing all day just because I've got a bird on my back. You should look where you're sitting, gurgle-gurgle-gloop." And with that he dived down and disappeared under the water, and so did Dodo.

For a moment her head popped out again. "Help! Drowning Dodo!" she bubbled, and was about to go under again when Mole-rat and Tilly splashed out to her and carried her back to shore. They tipped her onto the sand.

"What a mess I am now!" she moaned. "Just look at my soggy feathers! And I'd just got them looking nice again after being dragged through all those tunnels."

"Never mind, Dodo. You'll soon dry off. Lie down in the sand with Mole-rat and let the sun dry you."

"I don't suppose there's anything to eat

round here, is there?" Mole-rat sniffed the sand. "I've left all my food behind."

"What do you eat, Mole-rat?" asked Tilly.

"Bulbs and roots and things, deep in the soil," Mole-rat sighed, dribbling a bit with hungry memories. "And lovely juicy worms."

"I'll see what I can find," Tilly promised him. "But you stay here and watch Dodo, won't you? She looks tired out after all that excitement."

She clambered up a steep bank that led out of the little cove where Mole-rat and Dodo had stretched themselves out to sleep.

"Don't go away from there, will you?" she called to them. Dodo flapped her wing at her and waved her on her way.

Tilly went further into the jungle in her search for food. She was very hungry herself. She had no idea what a dodo might eat. The trees were heavy with all sorts of fruit, and as she reached up to pick some, Tilly saw a flying-squirrel leap off one high branch onto another tree.

"Wheee!" it shouted. "Wheeeee!" Another one cast off after it. "Wheeeeeeeee!"

They perched together on a branch and looked out across to the little cove where Tilly had been. More and more of them clustered on the branch, pointing to something far out to sea. They seemed to be saying something urgent to each other, and what they said came down like a whisper in the air, and seemed to be taken up again and floated off by humming insects, and drifted down again and whistled softly by slow-flying birds.

The further Tilly went into the bushes the greater the fluttering and whispering grew, till it seemed that the air of the island was buzzing with the same sad song: "All the poor dodos . . . all the poor dodos . . . all the poor dodos . . ."

"What do you mean?" Tilly shouted. "What's happening?"

A blue-green bird with golden eyes and a voice like a bell flew down and fluttered its wings rapidly so it hovered just over Tilly's head.

"Danger around. Danger everywhere," it chimed. "Pirate ship sailing. Beware. Beware . . ."

"A pirate ship!" Tilly dropped all the fruit she'd been gathering.

"Get back to her!" the chiming bird urged. "Back to her!"

Tilly ran back to the cove, pushing her way through the trailing bushes, her breath throbbing in her throat. Far out on the horizon she could see the riggings of a tall sailing ship. But when she came to the edge of the little bay she could only stand, helpless, staring at the place where Dodo and the mole-rat had been lying.

Because both of them had gone.

Chapter Nine

The World Belongs to All of Us

Dodo had been the first to go. As soon as Tilly had gone in search of food she opened her eyes and stretched herself. "Mole-rat," she said.

He snored and turned over.

"Mole-rat. Have all the dodos really gone?"

He snored again, rubbing his paw across his eyelid as a fly balanced there.

"I have to know," said Dodo. "I have to know if it's really true." Her voice was low and clucking. She pecked his head to try and wake him up. He tucked his paws round his ears.

"Then I'm going to find out for myself," she said.

She took a run at the bank, wishing she could just spread out her wings and fly up like any normal bird. The sand was soft and deep, and she kept sliding down again, but at last she made it to the top. With her last little flurry the fine sand sprayed behind her and showered like drizzle into Mole-rat's open mouth.

He jumped to his feet and looked round, blinking, not knowing at first what had woken him up, and then with a terrible panicky dawning of dread he realized that he had been asleep, and that he'd lost Dodo.

"Dodo! Dodo!" he wailed. He ran frantically in larger and larger circles. His long life underground had given him very poor eyesight; he could only really follow smells, or very clear tracks when they were right under his nose. But the sand was all scuffed up, and the smells were everywhere. He could just trace his own pawmarks, and then the marks left by Tilly's shoes, and at last, just when he'd given up hope and knew he'd have to go back down the tunnel for the queen's punishment, he found clawmarks in the bank.

He lunged up the hill, crazy with guilt. Dodo's tracks led him into the jungle, and then, as the undergrowth grew thicker, they disappeared. "Now what? Now what?" he shouted. His whiskers quivered. "I'm a stupid old mole-rat. I should never have been allowed to look after Dodo. I'm not fit to be given a job like that." He rushed into the foliage, sniffing for any scent that might help him. "Think! Think, you old fool," he told himself. He splayed his legs out and sank down, and almost immediately jumped up again. "The dodo's nesting-place!" he shouted. "That's where she'll be."

And that was where he found her, sitting with her head down and her beak tucked into her wing. Around her were scattered a few twigs and sticks, all that remained of the dodos' nests. Tiny fragments of eggshell glinted in the earth.

Dodo didn't look up when he tiptoed over to her.

"You won't find any dodos nesting here," he said to her gently. "They've all gone, Dodo. Really. They've all been killed."

She was making a low, brooding, froofy sound in her throat. "I had to find out for myself, Mole-rat. Just to make sure."

He nodded. "I know. Come on now. We'll have to get back to Tilly. She'll be terribly worried, you know."

Tilly stood at the top of the bank, gazing down at the place where she'd last seen Dodo and Mole-rat.

I'll never see them again, she thought. She felt a feather tickling her leg, and realized that they were standing right next to her.

"Where've you been?" she shouted.

"Oh, nowhere," said Dodo. "I wanted to go for a little walk, and, naturally, Mole-rat came too."

"I was worried about you, Dodo," said Tilly, crouching down to her. "I thought something was after you."

"There's usually something after me,"
Dodo agreed. "I'm very popular."

"Don't be silly, Dodo." Tilly wasn't in the
mood for laughing at Dodo now. "Why can't
they leave you alone?"

"I don't think they ever will."

"Then it's not fair," said Tilly. "It's just not
fair. The world belongs to all of us."

"The great of us, and the small of us,"
Dodo agreed sadly. "But some people just
don't seem to want to share it."

"But it's your world too," Tilly said.

"I know," Dodo nodded. "And I like being
here." She patted Tilly's hand with her wing.
"One day," she said. "One day, people might
understand that."

And it seemed to Tilly then that Dodo
wasn't a funny, stupid bird any more, or that
she ever had been really, but that she was
trying hard to shake away a real, deep
sadness that only hunted animals know
about.

"Tilly," said Dodo. "I want you to listen
very carefully. I've got a present for you.
It's a very special present. I want to give
it to you very soon, and I want you to
take it back home with you . . ."

"What do you mean?" asked Tilly. She felt suddenly sick with dread.

"Just listen. I want you to take it home, all the way back to England, and I want you to show it to all the children there. And to all the people who love animals. Oh, and birds, and fishes, and flowers, and trees. All the people who want to share their world with them. Will you do that?"

"Of course I will, Dodo. But I don't understand . . . I'm not going without you, Dodo. I'm not. I'm not!"

"I think you may have to." Dodo turned away. "I'll go and fetch it now." She waddled away into the trees again.

"Dodo! Come back!" Tilly shouted.

"It's all right, Tilly, I'll watch her. She'll be quite safe in the jungle," Mole-rat promised. He twitched his nose up, as if he was sniffing for danger. "This is where she must be careful, by the shore. You keep guard here. This is where you're needed."

"What do you mean?" asked Tilly, but Mole-rat only sighed, and shook his head, and cleared his throat a few times. "Don't set me off, Tilly," he said sadly. "You know what I'm like."

"But where's she gone now?"

"She's gone to a little clearing. A nesting-place. It's just up there. It's where . . . where . . ." He coughed and cleared his throat again. "Where the dodos used to lay their eggs. Only not now. Not now. None left, you see."

Tilly stared after her. "Go with her, Mole-rat," she begged. "Guard her. Please."

Mole-rat scrabbled up the sandy bank and followed Dodo back into the jungle.

Tilly sat down wearily. It would be lovely to go to sleep, she thought. To go back home and sleep. It was very warm on the beach, and the sound of the waves lapping on the sand was soothing and gentle. She closed her eyes to listen to it. But she must keep guard. She must!

Suddenly she heard the sound of voices across the water, sharp, heavy men's voices. She opened her eyes to see that it was beginning to grow cool and dark, and that there was a rowing boat pulling in to shore. Two men climbed out, one tall and one short; one old and one young. They hauled their boat onto the sand. One of the men held up a spyglass to his eye and peered round the island with it.

As soon as she saw their swarthy faces and rich clothing Tilly knew who they were. They were pirates. Never, never, had she felt so afraid.

Chapter Ten

The Song of the Dodo

The two men heaved their boat up onto the
shore. It rasped like sandpaper rubbing on
stone. When they stood up Tilly could see the
tallest one had a long, tufty black beard. He
strode across the sand in an angry mood. The
younger one, a lad, had to run to keep up
with him. Tilly crouched down and crept
backwards towards the cave. Keep away,
Dodo, she thought. Keep away!

Blackbeard began to shout angrily over his
shoulder. "What Godforsaken land is this,
brother? I'm hungry!"

"Have some fish!" snarled Pirate Lad,
handing him a raw steak of fish with a bite
taken out of it. Blackbeard slapped it out of
his hand.

"I think not, brother. I've had enough of
that stuff."

Tilly peered out at them from the shelter of
the cave, hardly daring to breathe.

Pirate Lad stopped and sniffed, turning his

head from side to side. He beckoned to Blackbeard. "D'you smell what I smell, brother? There's dodo in the air!"

"Oh no!" gasped Tilly.

He dropped down onto his knees to examine the sand. "And look at this! Dodo tracks!"

Blackbeard leaned down over him, and nodded slowly.

"What wouldn't I give, brother, for a dish of dodo stew! Swimming in gravy!"

Pirate Lad stood up and spat into the sand.

"Dodo stew's like vomit, brother!"

Blackbeard thrust his face close up to Pirate Lad's, his beard like a bristly brush scratching his cheek. They looked angry enough to fight each other.

"Best food on earth, is dodo . . ." he argued, and, very faint, very far away, almost as if it was in Tilly's own head, came the sound of Dodo's voice: "Oh, thank you, sir! Thank you!"

"Stay there, Dodo," groaned Tilly. "Stay there, please!" The two pirates were standing stock still, straining to listen to the distant sound through all the stirrings of the jungle.

Then the first pirate said softly: "What sound would you say that was, brother? I

haven't heard that sound in months . . . but I'd bet you a purse of guineas that it's the cry of the dodo bird."

"How can it be!" Pirate Lad scoffed. "There's no dodos left. You've ate 'em all, I bet! They're all dead now, brother. They're extinct."

And again, as tiny as if it was only in her head, Tilly heard Dodo's voice. "They don't stink."

Completely forgetting her own fear of the pirates, Tilly stood up and shouted as hard as she could.

"Run, Dodo! Run! Run for your life!" And as she said that the beasts and the birds of the island sent up their clamour, a deafening roar like mountains breaking open. They flapped their wings and leapt into bushes and crashed through trees, all to hide the sound of Dodo coming back towards the shore, and to cover up the sight of her yellow feathers in the dusk.

"Go away, Dodo!" Tilly screamed, and all the creatures screamed it with her. "Run!"

Tilly started to run up the fine sand at the side of the bank that would take her up to Dodo. Blackbeard grabbed her and hauled her back down again. The pirates stood each side of her, and hissed at her, one down each ear, as if they were singing her a terrible mocking song:

"You know where that bird is!"

"You're hiding it from us!"

"She's the only one left! Leave her! Leave her alone!" Tilly begged.

"Then tell us where to find it—"

"Or we'll spoil your face!"

"No!" shouted Tilly. "She's the only dodo in the world."

"I'm here," came Dodo's voice, calm and quiet behind them.

All the crying and clamour of the creatures died away to nothing. The pirates froze, with their arms held up to strike, like statues. Day had drained away into moonlight.

Dodo stepped forward. She held an egg in her folded wings, and she nodded to Tilly to come and take it from her. And in a voice that was as soft as a whisper, Dodo sang her the only song she knew; the song of the last dodo.

"This is the egg
The golden egg
The special egg from long ago.
Take it back to England
For children there to know.

For children who love animals
In air, on earth, in sea,
Who keep the forest places
For creatures to roam free
For children who let flowers grow,
And butterfly, and bee,

Who leave the fishes in their stream
And leave the spiders on their web
And leave the birds' eggs in their nest
And leave the beetle on its log.

This lovely, living planet
Belongs to every thing
That moves and breathes upon it;
A song of life I sing.

So take this egg
This golden egg
This special egg from long ago

And keep it safe
In memory
Of the life
And death
Of the last dodo."

Chapter Eleven

In Memory

Tilly knew then that this was the last time she would ever see Dodo.

She tried to rush forward to hug her but all the jungle creatures closed in a ring round Dodo and the pirates, keeping Tilly back so she couldn't see what was happening.

All the mole-rats came up from their burrows, led by their red-eyed queen. The lizards slid out from under rocks and stones, and the snakes slithered through the grass. Monkeys swung across the branches, and flying squirrels leapt into the air after them, and grey hooded birds swooped down, and red fire-birds, and insects with starlight on their wings, and all kinds of creatures that Tilly had never seen before, all clustering round Dodo and the pirates, all bowing their heads in silence.

For that was a terrible day, when the last of the dodos was killed by pirates, and it really happened, a long time ago.

And when the animals moved away, the pirates had gone. So had Dodo. All that was left of her was a handful of yellow feathers on the ground, swirling in the evening wind, and a sudden gust took them up and up, away over the trees, away over the island, into the floating path of the moon, so that for a second they looked like a yellow-grey bird in flight.

"Goodbye, Dodo," Tilly called.

And then they were gone.

But Tilly could hear the splash of oars on the dark sea, and the cruel laughter of the pirate brothers as they rowed back to their ship. Far out on the horizon she could see the pirate ship moored, with little lanterns swinging on it. She could hear the voices of men drifting across the water.

All the stars in the sky were reflected in the black, deep sea, and they were like the eyes of animals, cold and angry. Tilly was alone, and night was falling fast, fast all around her.

"I want to go home!" said Tilly. "Home! Home! I want to go home."

Then the wind of the night came rushing up to her, and lifted her as if she had no weight at all, and carried her like a leaf, or a balloon, or a bird's feather, or a speck of dream–dust. Voices kept coming to her, in and out of her mind:

"Best food on earth is dodo."

"Wait till I catch the dodo!"

"The world belongs to all of us."

"All the poor dodos."

"Dodos are like dinosaurs, they're all dead now" . . . over and over again in her mind, and then one voice kept coming through, stronger than the others, and closer than them . . .

"It's no good crying over dead dodos. Crying won't bring them back." She knew that voice.

"Mrs Hardcastle! Mrs Hardcastle!" she called.

Now she could see right down through treetops. She could see the surprised face of a badger peering up at her, and a hedgehog snuffling through leaves. She could see a mouse stretching out its back legs, and a rabbit nibbling lettuce leaves. Day was just starting. She was looking down inside the biggest tree in the forest, a huge chestnut tree with white flowers like Christmas-tree candles on its branches. And there was Mrs Hardcastle, yawning and rubbing her eyes as if she was just waking up from a sleep.

"Mrs Hardcastle, Mrs Hardcastle!" Tilly could hear her own voice, far away as if it was in a dream. "Oh, Mrs Hardcastle! I want to tell you . . . the island, and the big hunters . . . and the pirates came . . . oh . . . and the dodo, Mrs Hardcastle. The dodo. Did it really, really happen?"

And though she was whirling round so fast now that she couldn't see Mrs Hardcastle any more, she could hear her voice, as close to her ear as if she was up in the sky next to her . . .

"Yes, it all really happened, Tilly. A long, long time ago. Tell the children, Tilly Mint. Tell the children . . . Captain Cloud will help you . . ."

And Mrs Hardcastle's voice grew fainter and fainter, and the whirl of the wind tossed Tilly gently till she felt as if she was being rocked in a little boat on a lapping stream, and she could hear the sound of someone singing about jelly fish . . .

"Proper little squelchy things
Blobs of slime
Pink and purple bubbles,
Like dancers in the brine . . ."

and she knew that any minute now the

rocking would stop and she would come up with a bump against the wall of Captain Cloud's boat shed.

The jolt made her open her eyes. It was her bedroom door being opened. She was lying in bed, with Mr Pig tucked under the pillow and the sun warm on her through her window.

"Awake at last!" Mum laughed. She sat on Tilly's bed. "What a night it's been, Tilly! All that wind! And you didn't sleep very well, did you? I heard you shouting out for Mrs Hardcastle."

Tilly stared out of the window. She was sure . . . sure . . .

"Tilly," said Mum gently. "Mrs Hardcastle isn't going to come back again. You know that, don't you?"

Tilly nodded.

"I went round to her house last night," Mum said. "I wanted to help her brother to clear out her attic. And we found something that we thought you'd like to keep. You were fast asleep when I brought it in, Tilly. So I put it there for you. Look. On your special shelf."

"The egg! It's my egg!" Tilly gasped. She jumped out of her bed and ran to her shelf. She kept all kinds of special things there, like a conker, and a blue feather, and a bag full of sparkling dream-dust. And in the middle now was an egg, big as a golden melon, and yellow with age. She picked it up carefully.

"Captain Cloud thought you'd like it," said Mum. "I don't know what it is though. Do you?"

"Yes," said Tilly. "It's a special egg. A magic egg from long ago."

She put it back, very carefully, on her shelf.

I'll keep it safe
In memory
Of the life
And death
Of the last dodo.

"Mum," she said, "I want to tell all the children about the dodo. D'you think Captain Cloud would help me?"

"I'm sure he would," said Mum.

After breakfast Tilly went to Captain Cloud's house, and she told him the story of the last of the dodos.

"That's a very important story, Tilly Lizard," he told her when she'd finished. He stroked his beard thoughtfully. "I'll tell you what. I'll fetch you some paper and a pencil,

199

and we'll make it into a book, shall we?"
And this is it:

It was a very windy
night; the sort of
night that sounds
as if wild animals
are roaring round the
house and pawing at
the door to be let in

DOGSPELL
Helen Dunwoodie

*"Look, this is just what we need!
'Bring your dream to life.'"*

Daisy and Robina are two sisters
with one wish – to have a dog.
When they find a book of magic
that promises to make their dream come
true, they can't resist trying the spell.

When the girls return home later on,
a fabulous surprise awaits them. Dad
may have a boring explanation for it,
but Daisy and Robina think it's
truly enchanting!

A delightfully magical story about
wanting a dog.

ISBN 0552 548537

FUNNY FRANK
Dick King-Smith

*"I've got a chicken that wants to
be a duck!"*

Frank is a funny chick. Unlike all his
brothers and sisters, he doesn't want to
peck around at anything and everything
in the dust. No, Frank wants to dabble
about in the lovely duckpond, splashing
himself with water. Most of all, he
wants to learn to *swim*.

Can Jemima, the farmer's daughter,
find a way to help Frank? And if Frank
can swim like a duck, what will happen
when he grows up to be a cockerel?

A hilarious new tale from the master
of animal tales, Dick King-Smith,
creator of *Babe*.

'Sparkling humour and wonderful characters
are Dick King-Smith's trademarks'
Books for Your Children

0 552 547484

BUMBLE
Alison Prince

*"He's got a big bum. Why don't we
call him Bumble?"*

Bumble the hamster belongs to Rosie,
and he knows it's his job to keep her happy.
He entertains her with Pocket Diving, Ear
Tickling and Finger Balancing. But when
he tries Hide and Seek, Rosie's parents panic
and insist Bumble has to stay in his cage.
Rosie still feeds him delicious things, but
Bumble's getting bored – and fat!

Then mice arrive in the house. Rosie's
parents are horrified, Rosie isn't happy – and
Bumble is frantic. If things go on like this,
he'll lose his job. He has to come up with a
plan, and quickly…

ISBN 0552 54700 X

MR MUMBLE'S FABULOUS FLYBROWS
Jamie Rix

"Is it a bird?" "Is it a plane?"
"No. It's a man with incredibly large eyebrows!"

Mr Mumble has the largest pair of eyebrows in the world. One day, a passing tornado lifts his eyebrows and gusts him skywards like a feather. Mr Mumbles now has flybrows! They whisk him round the world on a whistle-stop tour but how is he to get down? His flybrows are out of control ...

Find out how Mr Mumble tames his flybrows and finds his way home in this hilarious story from the author of *One Hot Penguin*.

ISBN 0 552 547476

PIGFACE
Catherine Robinson

Pigface had never been anything other than Pigface. It was simply the perfect name for him.

Noah and his friends have always called the quiet, podgy boy in their class 'Pigface'. He is round and pink, and he lives on a pig farm, so he must know it's a joke, mustn't he? At any rate, Noah is sure he's never heard Pigface complain.

Then a new boy joins the class and Noah begins to wonder if nick-names are quite so funny after all...

A thought-provoking story about bullying at school.

ISBN 0552 54860X

THE SHRIMP
Emily Smith

Wild life!

Ben spends the holidays with his nose in
the sand and bottom in the air. It's not
because he's shy – though some of his
classmates do call him the Shrimp. It's
because he's got a great idea for his
wildlife project.

A competition is on! The class projects
are going to be judged by a famous TV
wildlife presenter, and the prize is irresistible.
Ben would love to win it, but others have
their eyes on the prize too…

ISBN 0 552 547352

SLEEPOVERS
Jacqueline Wilson

Sleepover parties are the greatest!
Everybody's having one…

All of Daisy's friends in the Alphabet
Club – Amy, Bella, Chloe and Emily –
have had sleepovers for their birthdays.
Daisy has a dilemma. She'd love to have
a sleepover too, but then she'd have to let
her friends meet her sister…

A funny and moving story for younger readers
from the award-winning author
of Lizzie Zipmouth and Double Act.

'Very readable… touching… Altogether,
this is Wilson at the top of her form'
Kids' Out

'Highly entertaining'
Times Educational Supplement

'Has all the Jacqueline Wilson hallmarks
of humour, good sense and a profound realism'
Independent

ISBN 0552 547093